JUDGE ALVIN WONG

MATT SHEA

Cover design by Renée Klause

Published in the United States of America ISBN: 978-1-62137-957-7 (softcover).

1. Fiction / General
2. Fiction / Small Town & Rural
16.09.26

This book is dedication to Jan!

True to form, our Jan naturally blends in with everyone.
Here she's captured, almost front and center wearing a white top, with her
ever-present smile. Another fantastic Christmas!

To Jan!

I'm proud to say that Jan Shea has been winning her battle with cancer! Her courageous battle has inspired all of us and made everyone take a closer look at the gift of life.

The story you are about to read depicts having a second chance at life, with hope and prayer being a definite factor.

Jan, you did your part in allowing our prayers to be answered, and we'll always love you for that!

Love, Matt

A SPECIAL THANKS TO
RENÉE KLAUSE!

Renée sitting at the desk of the Burien Art Gallery during her shift. Writing a report and pricing one of her abstract floral paintings.

For a second time, she has utilized her brilliant artistic skills and crafted a cover that perfectly represents my story line. The first was *The Meadowdale Community Project* (a book that was actually dedicated to her). That, along with her strategic input including many pictures, has assisted me periodically throughout my writings.

If you would like to see more of her artistic ability, which includes modern abstract and impressionism, you can contact her on Facebook under:

Artistic Xpressions by Renée Klause and thru
www.artistsunitedclub.com

Renée, thank you for another job well done!

Matt

It's Not A Party Without Ric!

My friends and I have always listened to "This Week In America" whenever the opportunity presented itself. One reason for our devout loyalty was based on the wonderment of what legendary radio talk show host, Ric Bratton, was going to do next. His show is only predictable when it comes to airtime, but from there—watch out!

We would listen to his traditional "larger-than-life" introduction with great anticipation. We would then begin to guess what icon he might interview, what cause he would possibly serve—or if he discovered another unknown whose story was about to be told, an "only-in-America" success story where someone's life was about to change forever with a dash of fame guaranteed.

There's far more to our man, Ric:

He has received numerous awards throughout the decades from both radio and television. Among other things, his jubilant personality served greatly as he was master of ceremony for Orlando Florida's *Ms. American United States Pageant*. There are also many worthy causes that deserve mentioning, such as being a chapter president for St. Jude Children's Research Hospital for twenty-eight years and being their 1990 Man Of The Year.

He did all of this while being the longest-running and highest-rated radio personality in America.

It is our honor to grab hold of Ric and take him a *different* direction. We have gone beyond adopting him as friend and family. This time, he has been kidnapped and incorporated as a character throughout this book! It is what we consider to be a 'brilliant move' that guarantees to keep the good times rolling with values in check. Ric, yer *totally awesome,* and we love you!

Your friends from the West Coast:
Laura, Ella, Renée and Matt

ACKNOWLEDGMENTS

What about Ella?

Ella Jane Ray (yes—*that Ella*) has been my "right-hand man" ever since my first publication.

It all started years ago when the apartment next door was vacated—and I prayed to get a decent neighbor.

Prayers do get answered! I was gifted a 'natural friend' who was the perfect fit to read my manuscripts to. A friend who loved the old Alfred Hitchcock and Twilight Zone reruns, liked spur-of-the-moment road trips and a good hamburger. In essence, she was truly a godsend and just what the doctor ordered!

Everything I have published so far has been thoroughly proofread and fine-tuned with Ella's steel-trap mind and great humor. Often, the midnight oil burned long until daybreak. I can honestly say that I would not have found the path I discovered in writing if it wasn't for my pal, Ella.

Ella, ya did it again, and we got this book done. Let's hit the road, and lunch is on me!

Matt

PROLOGUE

———●●●———

A dry, howling wind is ravaging the sunbaked prairie.

In the midst of its blistering destruction, a lone tumbleweed bounces. The dried-out vagabond scurries about, mindlessly skipping over dirt, stone, and brush. Within its awkward silence, it keeps rolling in an unorthodox path, stumbling precariously while at the mercy of nature. It is inevitable that the disregarded weed will eventually deteriorate into dust and dissipate in the unforgiving winds—only to be forgotten.

Ironically, the dried bush's wayward path personifies a life in the very town it is passing through—one that is being stripped of a false image held for decades. It is high noon, in a settlement known as Hangman, with a modern-day showdown about to start.

Our setting continues where the very tracks left by the town's first settlers can still be seen—parallel grooves that stretched across the plains, through the mountains, and off into infinity. In town, the main drag shows telltale signs of its proud heritage. This ranged from original storefronts with their wooden sidewalks- to hitching posts that stood the test of time.

True, advance technology does throw in a few tidbits like paved roads and electricity to this frontier community. Lest no forget however, that this township is always just one storm away from being thrown back over one-hundred-fifty years.

On more than one occasion it has.

Our story begins inside the town's courthouse where its path through history has always been defined.

CONTENTS

1

---•●●•---

Dusty beams covered a floor that resembled a cat's scratching post. Resting on the frayed wood was a series of benches that matched the pews across the street. Collectively, they faced a platform that bolstered the state's flag on one side and the stars and stripes on the other. Perfectly centered was an oak desk with a Bible and a law book in plain view.

It was there where a composed Judge Alvin Hershel Wong sat.

***

Alvin was the town's first nonwhite citizen. Standing at five-foot-seven, he was of a traditional Asian descent. His short, black hair was combed back, allowing the natural beauty of his heritage to prevail. High cheekbones and intense dark eyes showed perception surrounded with intelligence. A grand smile illustrated compassion for his fellow man. He was a credit to the black robe he wore.

It would be an understatement to say that there were many selling points to this forty-six-year-old judge. One was his easygoing demeanor that would brighten anyone's day. Another was his informal approach to serving justice. Often, he was affectionately referred to as 'Judge Alvin'. Typically, the good man always inaugurated a suit by gathering all who were involved and initiating a listening session. Often, such procedures resulted in old friendships being rekindled with a barbecue to follow. He was clearly a godsend, who listened with his modern-day ancient wisdom.

***

Silence continued to rule the proud landmark fueled by firewood and lanterns. If this stalemate were to go on any further, an eerie

1

sensation would certainly unfold; the portraits of past judges and governors would give one the feeling that he was being watched.

This hall of justice had its moments when one could hear a pin drop. It was also known to change in a heartbeat—becoming a volatile echo chamber. Those present remained calm as they matched eyes with the good judge.

More time passed...

In bewilderment, Judge Alvin finally spread his arms as if to say, *"Okay, who wants to go first?"*

One by one, all heads turned to an imposing figure sitting up front. The broad shoulders and thick neck needed no introduction. It was the plaintiff, Blaine Harold Wolf.

***

Blaine Wolf was a fifth-generation rancher. The Wolfs were among those who initially homesteaded in this town. Blaine's last name and imposing figure made him dignified. He was big in stature, standing at six foot four and tipping the scales at over 270 pounds. Wavy, sandy-blond hair matched the weathered face and wild blue eyes that hinted of someone who stayed focused and never backed down from a confrontation. His overbearing baritone served as an additional tool used by the forty-one-year-old man to force his way through life.

The man was also married with two children, who seemed to be stranded on an island. Socially, the price paid for living on the outskirts of town with their father's overbearing character. The man who wouldn't allow his pretty wife to have a driver's license. Outside of school activities, the family usually restricted their social activities to the company of relatives.

***

It was time to get the show on the road, with Alvin gesturing to Blaine to speak first. Tension mounted as the big man wearing a white cowboy shirt stood up.

Using his firm, rumbling voice, Blaine addressed the judge. "Do you want me to take the stand?"

"No, where you're standing is just fine," replied Alvin. "Now tell us what's bothering you, Blaine."

The notable rancher looked down to gather his thoughts. With eyes closed, he involuntarily clenched his fists while searching for the right words to say. A few more seconds passed, then he stood tall and began to plead his case. "I have always considered myself to be a fair businessman," he said. Alvin was relieved that his opening statement was delivered in a polite manner and nodded with approval.

It was there where the tempo changed. Blaine became more assertive and raised his voice a bit. The room was now an amphitheater, with everyone witnessing the tenacity of Blaine Wolf.

The cattleman went on to explain about the business arrangement he had with Gavin Woodley—and how he failed him. "I paid him a man's wage to do a man's job," Blaine said with conviction.

***

Gavin Woodley was a polite, harmless man who was loved by everyone. His tall, lanky frame was dressed in the traditional blue coveralls and red flannel shirt worn by his forefathers. His dark-brown hair and eyes were accented by his signature smile. He was a farmhand during the harvest season and transported livestock as a side job. He was known for being an honest, reliable worker who always arrived early and had the time of day for his neighbors.

A closer look shows that there was more to this man than his graceful presence; he was also the consummate family man who came home every night. Gavin, along with his wife, Tammi, and their nine-year-old twin daughters, Mary and Tanya, were involved with practically every community service the town offered and never missed their weekly church services. Gavin was that dad who would gladly play any role in a school play and who gives out the best candy on Halloween.

Gavin was deeply respected by all, because he loved everyone, but it was the Lord and his family who came first.

***

It was obvious that Judge Wong's desire to resolve the situation in a neighborly fashion would not take place. Blaine Wolf was far too arrogant for that. The big man would much rather prefer a public display.

From there, Blaine continued to strategically assassinate the character of the defendant up one side and down the other. Mild insults, analogies, and for-instances were all used as tools to further embarrass his hired hand.

Finally, the rancher seemed to be satisfied with the payload he delivered and quietly said, "That's all I can think of." Blaine Wolf sat down with the courthouse, digesting his wrath.

"We'll take a five-minute break," announced a disappointed Judge Alvin. A soft shuffle of feet could be heard as everyone left their seats to prepare for the second half.

What was meant to be five minutes was more like twenty. Regardless, in time, all were in their original seats, with Gavin Woodley on deck. It was now Gavin's floor, as Judge Alvin Wong motioned to him to stand up.

Without hesitation, the wholesome country boy stood up. In a quiet, clear voice, he began to speak. "I have always appreciated working for Blaine Wolf, and as far as I'm concerned, he has always been good to me. In regards to the record, I do owe him two hundred dollars. Let me explain."

Gavin continued to speak freely, using his hands and facial expression.

"I do miscellaneous work for Mr. Wolf that ranges from maintaining his property to hauling livestock. He has always paid me two hundred dollars in advance whenever he sold cattle to a meat company. This was so that my truck would be serviced and ready to go."

The thirty-two-year-old worker had more to say. "Up until now, our business has always worked out, until my truck broke down. I contacted him the moment it happened to let him know the situation. Blaine stressed that he had a deadline to make and paid another trucker to transport his livestock from my trailer to theirs. He paid them the same rate I was getting paid, so I do owe him a refund from the last load."

Lowering his head, he volunteered defeating news. "The problem is that I don't have the money now, but I will in another month." Gavin looked over to the man he worked for and proposed an offer. "As I said before, I'd gladly work it off on your ranch."

The entire courtroom, including Judge Alvin, was greatly impressed with Gavin. Everyone, that is, except for Blaine Wolf and a somewhat-obscure relative who had accompanied him.

***

It is popular theory that all families have that odd member who can be a source of embarrassment. In the case of the prominent Wolf family, things were no different, for Blaine's nephew, Grant, was sitting alongside him. The family member who definitely fit the bill. The partially-hidden twenty-year-old was allowed to attend

4

that day *if he promised Uncle Blaine that he would remain quiet.*

***

Grant Wolf was an enthusiastic young lad who held no interest in sports. In fact, he had few friends to speak of and was content to stay at home and watch old detective shows. True, he was clearly a Wolf, with his blond hair and striking blue eyes, but he showed interest only in things like drama and literature. He led the sheltered life of a boy who was the farthest thing from being a cowboy and who never held a girl's hand. He even possessed a butterfly net, with reports of using it.

Grant was a harmless problem child for Blaine's sister, Donna, because he was out of his element. The question was: what was his element? One day, his mother asked him what he wanted to be when he grew up. Like Jethro Bodine, who wanted to be a brain surgeon, he had an answer: Grant wanted to be a high-profile FBI agent like the ones on Criminal Minds.

All of this came from a struggling student who never pursued any form of higher education. The outcast who was lacking the single accomplishment needed to be labeled an idiot savant.

***

Alvin looked at Blaine and motioned with his fingers as if to say, "Well, what do you think about Gavin's offer?"

Blaine began to stew over the battle he would rather have. To him, Gavin's suggestion was just too easy.

Alvin dropped his arms in frustration and looked at the audience. "Does anyone have any ideas?" he called out. There were no takers, which set the stage for Grant Wolf. The well-behaved nephew stood up and looked at his uncle in hope that his leash would be extended.

Blaine didn't know what to think. True, he briefly explained to him what the case was about, but didn't know if the boy was up to anything. All he knew was that his nephew asked a lot of questions that week and brought a briefcase for whatever reason. Realizing that those present were at a minimum and that the hearing was almost over, he justified giving clearance.

It was the biggest moment in Grant Joseph Wolf's life. A dream coming true! He was now on center stage and on prime time. With a confident look of determination, he spread his arms for all to see as he walked up to the bench.

Standing just a few feet away from Alvin, he asked in a high pitch, *"Justice?"* He turned around with authority and faced those sitting- as to include them. "We are all here to find justice."

The entire town knew who Grant Wolf was and never questioned his good intentions. The good judge winked at Blaine with the understanding that his nephew would have to be pacified. Blaine returned a slight nod in appreciation. Grant went on to quote famous lines and clichés from television shows, amusing his audience. Finally he got into original material, making everyone lean forward and listen closely. With a perfect delivery, he said, "To have the defendant claim to be innocent would be like meeting someone who actually attended Woodstock- but never mentions it."

Grant knew from watching television, that it was time to pause and let his point sink in.

Alvin's face contorted as he watched eyes roll throughout the room. It was obvious that many have survived a situation where a loudmouth felt the need to display the *Woodstock Card*. The room began to question if Grant was actually going somewhere with his presentation and was willing to hear more. The misfit knew that he was on a roll and methodically marched forward.

Grant continued with his unorthodox style by throwing in another example: "It would be like arriving at a crime scene and forgetting to bring an ample supply of luminol." The detective shows taught society what that product was, and sadly, it didn't remotely apply to this case. Heads started to shake as people realized that their time was being wasted.

Grant seemed to have done his homework and came prepared. In a last-ditch effort, he threw them a fastball: "Let's equate the plaintiff and defendant to the binding of two cultures. For example: if there was not an influx of Portuguese migrating to Hawaii, this instrument would have never been conceived."

Immediately, he stepped over to where he was sitting and pulled a ukulele out of his briefcase for all to see. Holding it high above his head, he slowly turned it from side to side, proclaiming: "If those two cultures didn't unite, the world would *never* have known who Herbert Buckingham Khaury was!"

All at once, everyone got out their cell phones and started to google the famous name from the past.

Grant continued to hold the instrument while folding his arms with pride. He watched his subjects frantically push keys to enhance their education. Within seconds, everyone was focused on a website that told about the man he mentioned with his familiar picture displayed.

Groans filled the room, with a dejected Grant Wolf calculating his next step. Alvin looked at Blaine's beet-red face with pity. The courtroom was becoming a mockery, with the uncle knowing that his nephew was just getting warmed up. Blaine knew that he had to act fast and made his move. "Okay, let's just forget the whole thing, and he can keep the money!" shouted the rancher.

Gavin immediately responded to Blaine's statement and cried out, "Blaine, I can pay you within a month. I can also work it off, starting this very moment."

"Just keep it!" yelled the stock grower. "We wouldn't even be here today if it wasn't for you!" Blaine Wolf had enough and stormed out of the courthouse, leaving a bewildered Gavin Woodley feeling shamed.

The ultimate wound was created: Blaine Wolf had successfully deprived a good man of his dignity in front of others. All over two-hundred dollars.

2

———— •●• ————

Sometimes a small town's judicial system reaches a dead end. Such towns are known to improvise with an alternative forum where justice can be achieved. In the town of Hangman, the Lazy Trail Saloon would be such a place. It was lunchtime, and those left in the courtroom unanimously agreed that it was time to cash in on the Dollar A Hotdog Day down the street.

It went without saying that the absence of Blaine Wolf and his nephew would promise good times.

***

The good judge had replaced his robe with his white good-guy cowboy hat. He, along with the husband and wife team of Gavin and Tammi Woodley and a few others, left for the town's hotspot.

There are many benefits to living in a small town; one of which is the business districts they are known for.

Hangman was no exception, having everything within walking distance. From the steps of the courthouse, one could wave to a friend spotted entering the legendary saloon. In moments, Alvin and his party were in front of the frontier gin mill turned bar and grill; the only building in town that sported a few bullet holes and remained open past midnight.

Despite the many horror stories that encompassed its history, the establishment had been tame for decades. In fact, it was now the most fun place in town that offered a section where families could enjoy a good pizza and celebrate birthdays.

Alvin pushed his way through the western-style shutter doors and entered with his friends. In the far corner window, a vacant booth with plenty of seating seemed to beckon to them. "We got here just in time," said Alvin. Hats were immediately hung on a brass coat rack that stood by the door, and soon all eight were seated.

It didn't take long for the prestigious judge to be detected. Sixty-six-year-old Edna O'Brien couldn't help but notice him and called out. "Judge Wong, it's so good to see you!"

Alvin had many good attributes, and being able to laugh at himself was one of them. "*Judge Wong?*" he asked. "You must be referring to that funny looking guy who wears the black robe. I'm afraid he was left behind in the courtroom. Here, I'm just Alvin..."

As always, the Chinese American won over the entire room, with laughter ensuing. The result? Many began to scoot their chairs around the booth, knowing that everyone was welcome.

In time, the table was covered with pitchers of iced tea and hot dogs, with every imaginable condiment there for the taking. Alvin wasted no time in dressing his bun with plenty of mustard and sauerkraut. Using both hands, he held his creation up high and exclaimed, "This is just like being behind home plate and watching my team play!"

Despite the hearing ending on a sour note, it was good character spawning humorous stories with ridiculous ideas that circulated. Everyone took turns sharing the spotlight, with more neighbors gathering around. In a simultaneous rhythm, the room became a constant rumble of laughter. Finally, seventy-year-old Buck Thomson asked Alvin a personal question that also served as a compliment: "How come a good man like you is still single?"

Alvin leaned back in his chair and, with the face of an angel, rolled his eyes saying, "Well..."

All remained quiet to hear his reasoning.

Finally, he sat up and looked at Buck. "We're guys, right?"

Buck was no stranger to Alvin's brand of humor and tried his best not to laugh. In a quivering voice filled with anticipation, he responded, *"Yes..."*

"Do you remember when there were shows like The Dating Game?" asked Alvin.

"I used to watch that show all the time on rabbit ears," replied the feisty old man with gray hair.

Alvin moved closer and lowered his upper body as if he was going to tell a secret. Whispering loud enough for all to hear, he asked, "Weren't those women beautiful?"

"They certainly were," agreed Buck. "I couldn't watch that show unless Becky was in the other room." The married man of fifty years forgot who he was sitting next to and received a sharp elbow below his ribs. Nodding husbands were also delivered a warning shot, with the topic allowed to continue.

9

"Then there was The Newlywed Game," said the bachelor. "Things seemed to change at that point because sometimes, a significant other would reveal an intimate secret to gain more points..." Standing up, he pointed at Buck and said, "There were episodes where you could see the embarrassment on their faces—just to win a set of Samsonite luggage!"

Those gathered recalled such airings and chuckled.

The table grew quiet as Alvin sat down and leaned back, placing his arms behind his head. He continued, "Then came Divorce Court..." Gesturing at the sky, he added, "They were all so young..." He pounded his fist on the table and elaborated further. "Then there were those who just wouldn't learn, and they ended up on Judge Judy!" Alvin winced over the destructive domino theory common in western relationships and covered his face.

Everyone was laughing hysterically.

Looking at his friends, he exposed his hands while admitting, "Hey, I'm not perfect either, but this guy is just fine staying home and ordering a pizza."

"I can see your point," said Buck as he received a second jab. "Ouch!"

No one ever accused Judge Alvin of being blind.

The lunch crowd was satisfied and thoroughly entertained. In time, it began to thin out with those choosing to hang with Alvin sticking around. It was then that the room encountered an astronomical mood swing; Blaine Wolf came in off the street. He was alone this time, and obviously hungry. In true gentlemanly fashion, Alvin got his attention and motioned him to sit at their table.

Blaine accepted.

Floorboards breathed with a mild chime from worn heel plates. Together, they grew louder as the massive soles approached where Judge Alvin and company sat. Blaine pulled out an empty chair, while acknowledging everyone and took a seat.

"It's good to have you here," said Alvin with a sincere tone.

"I appreciate that," replied Blaine. The big man found it difficult to talk because he was surrounded by the very faces he saw earlier that day. Despite all present being cordial, he still didn't know what to say.

It was Gavin who finally broke the ice. "Can I get you a hot dog?" he offered in a polite tone.

The act of kindness did not sit well with Blaine. The rancher turned to Gavin and in a calm voice, gave his response. "No, I can pay for my own..."

"Well, I can get another one down," said Alvin as he got the server's attention. In moments, a few more dogs were ordered, with another round of tea on the way.

Blaine continued to show signs of feeling uncomfortable throughout his meal. In time, he swallowed his last bite, looked at everyone and abruptly addressed the table. "Look," he said, "I know there are times when I look bad to everyone, but I just want it understood that I am law abiding and simply do what I think is right—just like everyone else here. I never mean to hurt anyone."

Gavin made another attempt to mend his relationship with the man who just tried to sue him. "At one time or another, we're all misunderstood a bit," he commented.

Immediately, everyone looked at one another while nodding in agreement. That moment made Blaine feel more accepted and less of a pariah. He began to loosen up and specifically addressed Alvin. "You probably don't even like me," remarked the cocky rancher with laughter in his voice. "That doesn't bother me a bit, though-because I'm used to that!"

"I don't have a problem with you," replied Alvin. "Unless you got the last hot dog!" Everyone laughed with Alvin, including Blaine.

The former plaintiff began to mellow and affectionately patted the judge on his shoulder. "I respect your fairness," he said. "I also realize that you are restricted by law and have your hands tied."

"What do you mean by that?" asked Alvin.

Blaine spread his arms with open hands and faced the public servant and explained in better detail, "You aren't allowed to actually sentence someone the way you'd like to. If you could, how would you sentence a guy like me? In fact, I grant you permission to give me any type of sentence you feel I'm deserving of, and I promise to carry it out in full."

"I still don't understand," remarked Alvin.

Blaine got more assertive. "What I am trying to say is that there is a bit of sense that comes from those small town sheriffs that have sentenced minor offenders from a barber chair. Those situations are quick and to the point, without any interference. I have always appreciated that approach the best."

"At this table, I am not a judge," said Alvin. "I am just *Alvin*."

Blaine continued to push his luck and essentially gave Alvin consent to sentence him right then and there—in front of half the town. "Show me right now how you would judge me if you were allowed to," he challenged.

"Okay, okay," answered Alvin, "if that's what you want..." He positioned his chair directly toward Blaine, realizing that the whole room was listening. "I need to ask you a few questions first."

"Shoot," said Blaine.

"What is your most prized possession?" asked Alvin.

It took Blaine a microsecond to respond. "My friends and family."

"Who would you consider to be your best friend?" asked Alvin.

Blaine knew that everyone was aware of the answer to that question. With pride, he identified who his best friend was: *Gary Harris*.

***

Gary Harris was arguably the most successful and respected man in the county. He was the equivalent of being what Blaine Wolf was as a rancher—including a stand-up reputation that wasn't limited to his trade.

Gary was handsome, with black hair parted off to one side. He was six foot even, with medium build, dark eyes and puritan light skin. He always walked with a smile and gave one the impression of being a preacher. Naturally, this package came with his charming wife, Penny, along with his son, Ben and daughter, Mary Beth. The children attended the local elementary school where their mother was a volunteer.

Gary was regarded for being a great family man and upstanding citizen who showed unlimited compassion for others. He served as an important friend who was not only allowed to see Blaine's good side, but who also gave that political pull that made him look better than he actually was.

The age-old adage about being judged by the company you keep applied here for Blaine Harold Wolf. One that actually enhanced his overall image a bit.

***

"I have another question," continued Alvin.

"Shoot," replied Blaine.

"What is the most expendable item that you can think of that he could afford to lose?" he asked. The Chinese American judge elaborated further: "Something that is useful to anyone, something that he has an excessive amount of. An item that he would never miss if he parted with *just one*."

Blaine loved the moment. He could now inadvertently brag

about how wealthy he and his best friend were. After all, it was well known that they were the two most successful ranchers in the county. Usually, the arrogant man had to resort to more subtle means to draw such attention to himself.

"Money," replied the smug rich man.

Alvin probed deeper. "Would he ever do you a favor?"

Blaine was insulted. "That man would do *anything* for me. All I would have to do is ask!"

Alvin questioned further. "Would he value your friendship to the point where he would be willing to part with one of his dollars if you asked for it?"

"He would do that without hesitation!" answered the defensive rancher.

"How about making this favor even less of a sacrifice by simply borrowing a single dollar for one day?" challenged Alvin. "Then you can give it back to him the next."

"Oh, forgive me," said Alvin as he excused himself. "I meant to say, *one dallah*."

That comment made Blaine blush with embarrassment. When Alvin first arrived in Hangman, Blaine anticipated broken English. With cruelty, he would mimic his rendition of how he thought the new judge would enunciate the English language, while the others laughed. Blaine looked up and uttered, "I'm sorry."

"That's okay," said the judge while leaning over and patting him on his shoulder. "We're all friends around here."

Blaine mentally got back on track and realized that Alvin had just issued him what seemed to be a petty assignment. "Is that my sentence?" asked the big man. "You only want me to borrow *a dollar* from my best friend and pay him back the next day?"

"Yes," answered Alvin.

Blaine sat back deep in thought. The task seemed too easy. Then his brash character took over. "Consider it done!" he said. "I will be back soon to show you the dollar, then I'll give it back to him tomorrow."

Blaine Wolf placed a twenty-dollar bill on the table; an oversized payment for all to see. A silent tactic used to emphasize that he had plenty. The proud man in the classy western outfit stood up like a gentleman. He departed graciously to the coat rack, put on his hat, tipped it to everyone and walked tall out of the bar.

Alvin's eyes remained focused on Blaine as he left. With pity, he slowly shook his head back and forth knowing what his future would hold.

Alvin knowingly played Blaine Wolf like a vintage type-writer.

The clever judge simply used what could be considered a pencil and placed the ribbon off its track. The overconfident rancher would blindly use his fingers in an attempt to position the ribbon back in place. Judge Wong knew that Blaine's ego would not allow him to foresee the consequences of permanent stains.

3

Blaine Wolf embarked to the homestead of Gary Harris. True, he was a bit perplexed over the two tier mission assigned, but realized he was better off just doing it. This direct approach would prohibit him from having to answer to the apprehensive eyes looking back in the rearview mirror. The self-assured man who never questioned what he had, approached the cutoff that led to the two most prosperous acreages in the valley. Without wasting time to signal, the white crew cab slowed down and swerved onto the dirt road, bouncing on the uneven terrain.

A sigh of relief always overcame Blaine Harold Wolf at this point. He was now in his own world, with the controversies surrounding his image left behind. To him, this was the end of the world, the very road his forefathers built to start their legacy. Furthermore, it was blessed by having his best friend as his only neighbor—a family that included a wife and two kids who meshed well with his.

One would have to ask, "How can a man with such a callous disposition be so lucky?"

The mighty 4x4 with dual wheels decelerated further and began the act of dodging chuckholes. It was there where his subject came into view. Directly in his sights, at twelve o'clock, was the all-terrain vehicle owned by his neighbor and best friend.

The awkward moment suggested a makeshift duel. Without hesitation, Gary Harris began to improvise and pretended to play chicken. Blaine countered by momentarily covering his face while displaying an expression of fear. Cautiously, each avoided the other and parked side by side. With engines idling and windows opened, Blaine fired first. "Hey, why don't you watch where you're going?"

Shaking a scolding index finger, Gary returned fire, "Who taught you how to drive anyhow?" The friendly taunting went for a few more rounds until Gary switched subjects. "Do you think it's time to grade the road again?"

Blaine looked up and down the wavy lane and commented, "I think so," a dark cloud seemed to cover him. The butterflies in his stomach were beginning to take its toll over the uncomfortable favor he was about to ask. It took a microsecond for his friend to detect that something was wrong.

"Is there something bothering you?" asked Gary.

Blaine's somber expression was accompanied with a bashful set of twinkling eyes and uncontrollable fidgeting. This prepared his friend for the worse.

"Look," he said in an unusually soft voice. "I hate to ask, but would you mind letting me borrow one dollar?"

Blaine immediately became defensive and tried to comfort his friend with assurance. "I promise to pay you back the first thing tomorrow!"

Without question, Gary unbuckled his shoulder harness and leaned forward. From there, he resembled a contortionist by reaching his right arm behind his back and retrieving a black leather wallet. A guilt-ridden Blaine Wolf watched the man he regarded so highly. It agonized him to see Gary go through the painstaking process of unexpectedly being hit up for money and mindlessly adhering to a friend's needs with currency that not only reflected his responsible life but served as testimony to his belief in his fellowman.

It was one of the most uncomfortable moments in Blaine's life as the sacrificial dollar exchanged hands. Expressing a touch of concern, Gary asked, "Is that enough?" Blaine blushed and lowered his head. Finally, he gathered himself and regained his composure. Looking at his friend, he spoke with a dry throat. "Thanks a lot, Gary. This is all I need, and you will get this back tomorrow, and then I will explain everything."

"Just as long as you're okay," he replied. Gary Harris continued with his gentleman-like deportment and acted as if nothing had happened. With ease, he put his truck in gear and saluted while driving off.

The man who was to be a dollar richer for one day did not feel right. It was obvious that the passing of the green-back brought with it an element of apprehension—one that constituted a "party foul." There was no doubt that Blaine's best friend and neighbor left feeling a bit peculiar and possibly disappointed.

True, there was a bright side to all of this. Blaine did prove that his friend would lend him a dollar. In fact, what seemed to be the toughest part of his sentence was fulfilled almost too easily.

It was now time to submit the evidence to the jury of his peers. Without wasting time, he would return to the Lazy Trail Saloon judicial system and show the prized dollar. What was more important was the relief he would find the following day. Things would be back in order with the debt being paid and all loose ends tied. Or so he thought...

4

The return trip seemed to take forever, despite some disregarded yield signs and high school driving. Making record time, Blaine was delighted to see that the vehicles initially parked out front remained untouched.

The man who wanted to be on trial made his grand entrance into the fabled landmark. Immediately, all eyes turned to the triumphant rancher who waved the legal tender for all to see. Blaine headed to the table where Alvin sat and placed the dollar before him. Utilizing a sarcastic tone, he pointed to the paper money and said, *"There!"* He then pulled out a chair and sat down.

Blaine Harold Wolf had formally made a proclamation: He proved beyond any doubt- that Gary Wilfred Harris was not only his friend, but *a very special friend.*

Judge Alvin and those remaining who witnessed the sentencing reciprocated by giving Blaine a standing ovation for his achievement.

To say that the brash, beefy man became riddled with embarrassment would be an understatement. Red crept all over his face as he displayed a look of bewilderment.

Blaine felt like a fool, but there was no laughter to worsen it. Mentally, he began to trace his steps backward to assess what went wrong. Finally, the would-be defendant who upheld his end of the plea agreement, questioned the judge. "Why did you suggest such a thing anyway?" Blaine's mind was racing fast, and he retracted what he just asked. "Never mind," he said, shaking his head. "I guess I'm supposed to figure that out on my own..."

Alvin picked up the tempo by paying Blaine a compliment. Leaning forward, the man who yielded one-hundred pounds playfully slapped his hand against Blaine's shoulder and said, "Everyone around here knows that you have a great friendship with Gary. That's because you're a good guy just like him." The comment registered, allowing the rancher to save face. "What happens now is between you and your friend," he added.

Blaine digested what was said and nodded to himself in agreement. Quietly, he took the dollar off of the table and folded it into his shirt pocket. Alvin shifted gears and reached for a pitcher of iced tea. Using both hands, he held it up to his face and squinted at it. "What's this I see?" he said with an amused, mystified tone in his voice. "Why, there seems to be a message inside here."

All present were amused as Alvin continued. "Oh, I see that it's ancient writings."

Laughter ensued on that side of the room. "It says, *Must be shared with Blaine Wolf.*"

Everyone laughed hard, including Blaine. A second ovation followed that was more politically correct. The man in the spotlight started to loosen up a bit and joined in by saying, "I'll drink to that!"

Everyone sat down.

The table became festive as a final round was shared with the exchange of more stories. One by one, each patron bottom-upped and excused themselves until only Alvin and Blaine remained.

It was then that the ambiance of the Lazy Trail Saloon took an outwardly turn. In mid sentence, Blaine's ears detected what was to be interpreted as a warning. Alvin's radar was on the same frequency, as each closed their mouth to utilize other senses. The unmistakable jovial chatter of two well-known locals could be heard outside and was growing louder. Their keen senses quickly identified the unwanted entity that was drawing near, but it was too late. With no time to hide, each sat up straight with their hands resting in plain view on the table. Stomachs churned as Blaine looked at Alvin with a worrisome look that telegraphed they were in the wrong place, at the wrong time.

What was the saloon's worst case scenario had been identified and confirmed. Breaking through the western doors was a second dose of Blaine's twenty-year-old nephew, along with his tag-team partner, Marcus Hipple.

Can we say *butterflies*?

***

Mayor Marcus Stanley Hipple represented the cleanest of the clean.

The thirty-year-old, who stayed home on prom night, lived with his mother. A woman whose mere presence had him stand at attention. This milquetoast image was further cursed by the absence of a father who wasn't there to guide the feeble, premature-balding teen with awkward social skills. All of this while standing at five-foot-eight and wearing a fixed grin.

The result? A timid youth who survived school through the Science Department and Nature Club. A scarred boy who was denied friends and dined alone.

Hangman was a town that took care of its own by creating what was needed. For that very reason, Marcus Stanley Hipple had the surprise of his life when the township tipped the scales even after his incarceration in the public school system.

One day his mother answered a knock on the door, only to be greeted by the media and a bouquet of flowers. To her, it was no surprise that her "little angel" was appointed mayor by being a unanimous write-in. After all, who else was there to lead this town? In her mind, Marcus was clearly mayoral material and a bag of chips. Needless to say, his mother was proud beyond words and immediately hung the American flag on their front door.

As for the life of Mayor Marcus Stanley Hipple, the many years of rejection were made up for on that fateful day—a tribute to an innocent guy who was always picked on. One who never hurt a fly.

Marcus was now a figurehead in a self-running town. Still pitifully naive on many fronts and armed with corny jokes, he went steadfast to lead those who once mocked him. Or so he thought...

***

The square pegs entered the saloon, bringing their boisterous conversation with them. All those present, including Blaine and Alvin, knew what was in store.

"Did you see that *Danaus plexippus* gracefully fluttering by that Teleflora Pink Azalea plant?" projected an enthused Grant Wolf.

It was apparent that Grant noticed a monarch butterfly flying around a pink bush and felt compelled to tell the whole world about it.

"Oh, that must have been an amazing sight to behold!" replied the counterpart who wore a loud sweater with imprints of multicolored butterflies and sporty, beige pants.

Blaine leaned toward Alvin and whispered, "Whose idea was it to nominate him as mayor anyway?"

Alvin became defensive and retaliated. "I thought it was you!"

"Just remember that Grant is my sister's son, not mine," Blaine emphasized.

20

Judge Alvin was about to pay a price for his popularity. The well-conceived plan, devised by Marcus and Grant, would utilize the best vantage point the team could find as a means to divide and conquer. Today the corner table, where Blaine and Alvin sat, would suffice. From there, they strategically took empty seats on opposite ends while asking if they could join them.

"Sure, why not?" replied an accommodating Alvin. Blaine maintained his eye-contact as the good judge took a deep breath to prepare himself. Painted in a corner, the lepidopterists made their next calculated move, with Mayor Marcus Stanley Hipple poised to strike first.

Their goal?

To make yet another attempt to initiate a butterfly club in the town of Hangman.

Mayor Hipple raised his voice so that all could hear. "That *Rhopalocera* you saw may only have a lifespan of about twelve months, but with nearly twenty-thousand different species to savor; I just didn't know where to start!"

A customer within earshot became the first casualty and left for the bathroom.

The assault continued.

Motioning his hands for all to see, Grant addressed the entire room. "That's because everyone knows how exhilarating it is to watch their wings display vibrant colors in fields and meadows!"

Another patron got up to join the man in the bathroom. The uneven personalities that complimented one another kept going, tit for tat. Large, complex scientific words popped up frequently in hope to tantalize others to join in. Blaine Wolf saw that it was time for somebody to take a stand and dared, "Hey, have you guys ever thought about following bees and flies instead?"

Victory! Someone's curiosity was finally piqued, ensuring a question that could get the ball rolling. Marcus locked eyes with Grant. Together they nodded silently, realizing that the community had begun to give feedback. Though small; it was like a hardware store having its first sell be a ninety-nine cent screwdriver- it was a start!

Their faces showed a mixture of emotions however, for it was none other than Blaine Wolf himself who entered the conversation. His suggestion was indeed heard with its implications being fully digested. Initially, the thought of changing their course to focus on colonies of *Bombyliidaes* and *Disambiguations* did seem a bit odd. Marcus never lost sight that part of being a mayor was to be objective— meaning that Blaine's idea would have to be given some consideration. It was time to discuss the matter with the like-minded duo about to play the role of Siskel and Ebert. Everyone watched with great amusement as the former debate team captains from different eras began to joust. Huge scientific words that had never been heard before were enunciated flawlessly. Moments in history were also used to serve as example to further prove who was right, with index fingers pointing. The debate got so intense that the surrounding laughter went unnoticed.

Grant defended the *Calliphoridae* for having a keen sense of smell that could cover a mile. He went on to point out other life-threatening duties that the blowfly must perform or else the food chain would be disrupted. Marcus sat with his arms folded and remained calm as a cucumber. He followed Grant's logic and could only agree.

Without any notice, the mayor suddenly pointed directly at him, questioning if he forgot about the importance of *Apiformes*, even though they do not exist in Antarctica. He continued his momentum by cutting deeper, reminding that without them- there would be no honey.

Grant was mortified by the accusation and rebuked, "Oh heavens, no!"

A few more rounds of well-documented facts were used as arsenal, with no one understanding a single word of what they were talking about. Finally, the pair calmed down and agreed to do a visual of flies and bees. Next, they were to be compared to the picturesque butterfly. Immediately, a distasteful contrast came to mind as they looked at one another and slowly turned to Blaine.

It was obvious that whether the suggested insects had two or four wings, they were still transparent with virtually no color to speak of. Their black bodies, with or without yellow accents, could never compete with the patterns of any butterfly. Also, they were known to be very small, to the point where many considered them to be *too small*.

Furthermore, they would often dart like a laser beam and were never known to flutter like a flute hitting every note.

Their argument had them mutually agree on the importance of such insects; but where was the beauty? Both men were in a state of confusion, with Marcus having to ask Blaine an obvious question: "Why would you want to trade butterflies for bees and flies?"

Blaine's timing was impeccable. With the entire room waiting to hear his answer, he leaned inches away from the mayor's face and shouted. "So that the next time you come up with a stupid idea like that we can tell you to *buzz off!*" Backwash filled glasses as laughter shook the entire structure. Alvin was grateful that he recently used the restroom and doubled up in hysterics.

Marcus and Grant weren't quick enough to immediately grasp Blaine's brand of humor. Momentarily, each was at a loss for words until their recall had them realize that they had just been insulted. This prompted them to respond with a delayed reaction. Years of counseling taught them what to do in such a situation: *Show that you are strong enough to laugh at yourself like a politician.* They did just that and laughed like a foreigner trying to fit in at a cocktail party. They forced a phony laugh at the right time for all to hear— like a politician.

This was the perfect moment for Blaine to exit. He placed some loose change on the table and tipped his hat to Alvin, who still hadn't recovered from his laughing fit. It was time for the humorous cowboy to change scenery with a good cup of coffee in mind. This thought developed further when Blaine realized that he could have the best cup in town and visit with his oldest childhood friend, Ric Bratton. Blaine got in his truck and made a *beeline* to the Hangman General Store, where Ric's shop always had fresh java.

5

Ric Bratton shared a few similarities with Blaine Wolf. One being that their forefathers were the first to settle in Hangman. Though Blaine would claim that his family was the first to stake property, an honest Ric Bratton could disagree.

The man with vibrant silver hair and sensible eyeglasses, was never one to upstage another. Instead, Ric would take the time to understand *any* individual by knowing that we all have our shortcomings. Sometimes, a shortsighted person would fault him for being too nice. In time, such people faced hardships and thanked the Lord that there was a 'Ric Bratton' in their life.

His ever-present, big brother image set him aside from the other men in the valley. Every year he received the most Christmas cards, with everyone, regardless of from what walk of life, addressing him on a first-name basis. Everyone was family with Ric.

***

Blaine entered the store where his great-grandfather used to take kids for a sundae. The old brass bell on top of the door chimed instantaneously as the unmistakable aroma of Ric's signature coffee tantalized his senses.

"I hear you're a dollar richer today," greeted Ric as he poured coffee into Blaine's favorite mug.

"Now, how on earth did you know about that?" asked the bewildered rancher.

The shopkeeper chuckled with his reply. "Have you forgotten that we live in a small town?"

Blaine winced, remembering that in Hangman, news traveled faster than the Pony Express. The man who grazed the sides of most doors made his way to the small dining area, where one could enjoy tasty treats and visit with friends. As he was sitting down, his favorite mug was placed on a coaster and slid before him. "I suppose you won't let me pay for this," commented Blaine.

"Not if your last name is Wolf," replied Ric in a gingerly voice.

***

Ric and Blaine had roots that went back to the origin of the town they lived in. Regardless of whose story was told, both were of the families that establish the township of Hangman. There was more to the story.

It was wholeheartedly agreed upon by every local historian that Blaine's great-great-grandmother nursed Ric's great-great-grandmother for over a month while crossing the country. A touch-and-go, near-death experience that prompted last rites to be read. The gallant Margaret "Molly" Brown of the wagon train did win her battle against nature, thus preventing the extinction of the Bratton family line. An act of courage and selflessness that one Richard William Bratton will always honor.

***

Blaine could only thank him by raising the steaming cup in the air to toast their heritage: "To the wagon train."

"Amen to that!" responded Ric.

It was at that moment when Marsha Greene entered the store with her preschool daughters, Monica and Megan. The trio in matching pink and white outfits, joined hands and marched to the counter.

Ric was delighted to see the young family and called out. "Well, well, well; look who's here!"

The well-behaved children knew that it was okay to let go of their mommy and charged him with open arms. Jubilantly, they did just that, almost knocking the middle-aged man over in the process!

Ric was taken as he regained his balance. Laughingly, he looked down at the children hugging his knees. Looking up, he addressed the twenty-five-year-old mother and began to softly spell out their favorite desert.

"I-c-e c-r-e-a-m?"

The children were well aware of Ric's kindness. They also knew that when adults were talking in code, that usually meant a good thing. The girls looked at their mom in anticipation.

Soon, all three ladies were sitting at the counter on tall barstools. In a moment, three root beer floats topped with cherries stood before them. Over and over again, they thanked him. "It's my pleasure!" he replied with his enthusiastic demeanor. "Besides, that ice cream was getting close to being outdated, and I just can't see it going to waste." There was more.

Ric fully understood the plight of the single mother and those like her. In their honor, he reserved goods that were destined to be pulled off the shelves, and boxed them. These unmarked gifts were personally distributed to help anyone in need. "After all, it's a sin to waste," Ric would point out. Before leaving, Marsha held a private conversation with Ric as Blaine watched. After that, Ric went to his back room as the mother took her children to their car. Next, he carried two care packages outside and met her at his gas pumps. Blaine watched the good man place the boxes in the trunk of her car and close it. Then he began to pump gasoline—a time-consuming chore that must have topped off an empty tank. Once done, he leaned toward the open car window and wished the family well.

Ric was finally back in his store when Blaine shared a conclusion he arrived at. In a scolding tone, he said, "You're too nice."

Ric sat in front of his friend and digested the words. Repetitively, he tapped his chin with an index finger as he rolled his eyes asking, "Too nice? I've heard that comment before." Looking directly at the rancher, he asked, "Would you please tell me what being *too nice* means?"

Blaine took a long breath knowing that they were going to be there for a while. "Let's have some coffee over this," said Ric. A few customers drifted in and were promptly taken care of. Soon, two full mugs set the stage for a lengthy conversation between two old friends...

Blaine started first. "It's like the time when Doris Smith forgot to bring her lunch to school, so you shared yours."

Ric looked up to the heavens in a dream state and said, "Doris Smith...I remember that day very well." He then looked at Ric and commented, "Weren't we all hungry approaching lunchtime?"

"Boy, was I ever!" replied Blaine.

"Well, so was Doris," Ric pointed out.

Blaine leaned back and imagined what it would have been like to miss lunch and said, "I never would have survived that."

Ric leaned inches away from his friend and whispered, "She was my first kiss!"

"You got to kiss Doris Smith?" Blaine asked in awe. "I had a crush on her throughout school, and she had nothing to do with me."

"It was just one," said Ric. "It happened on the playground

during recess. From that day forward, we had a special friendship, but nothing further."

Blaine digested what Ric said and held his ground. "You still went hungry that day because of a mistake someone else made!"

"Don't we all make mistakes?" replied Ric.

"You would have been a millionaire long ago if you would simply let others fend for themselves!" Blaine barked.

"Sometimes the problem is through no one's fault. It's just bad luck." Ric elaborated a step further and struck a nerve. "Isn't that the beef you have with Gavin Woodley?"

Blaine momentarily lost control and dropped his fist on the table- Almost shattering his mug. "I was just trying to teach him a lesson!" he said.

On that note, he stormed out of the store muttering to himself. Ric was left behind feeling lousy. The humble shopkeeper wished he had never mentioned Gavin.

6

——•●•——

Blaine Wolf left the road to travel the path that led to his childhood home. It was now a ride down memory lane—one that divided the acreage of the county's two most successful ranchers.

Looking from side to side, he admired the matching white fences that outlined the properties. Rolling hills filled with trees, and green pastures could be seen as far as the eye could see. Scattered about were cattle grazing with an occasional pond where rainbow trout lived.

Up ahead was a fork in the road where matching wrought iron gates stood mighty and tall. The massive structures were accented with rusted wagon wheels covering each of its four corners. The gate on the right had the name 'Wolf' spelled out on top in rustic metal. The gate on the left had the name 'Harris'. Within view, each residence showed an early American ranch house that stood proud since the town was born. There were also corrals that allowed the families to spend the day riding horses together. On the Wolf side, stood four distinct breeds that represented each family member:

There was a beautiful light-brown Shetland pony with long white hair and a matching tail that seemed to come from a fairy-tale land. This showpiece belonged to the youngest in the family, Teri. Brilliantly, she matched beauty with class and named it after one of her favorite idols: Cher.

Next to Cher was Elvis—a white Appaloosa horse with black legs and spots. This was Junior's steed and like a sports car- had plenty of go!

Blaine and his wife, Stacey, were dyed-in-the-wool country folk. The majestic white Arabian horse with brown highlights was aptly named 'Annie Oakley'—a message to the wild West that the men had some competition.

Remaining was a golden Palomino with long white hair and a matching tail. Blaine's love affair with Roy Rogers had him search high and low to find what could only be named, 'Trigger'.

These traditional homesteads clearly served as testimony that one could have a piece of heaven—if they worked for it.

Blaine was well known for being rough around the edges. His temperament did however, subside briefly when he arrived home. His first greeting would come from his faithful dog, Blue. The loyal German Shepherd always brought out the boy in Blaine, bringing on a few minutes of fun-filled roughhousing.

Next, he would open the front door, knowing that Stacey would be there to hug the man she loved. The soft-spoken petite woman with lavish blonde hair and green eyes was obedient to a fault. Cheerfully, she asked, "How was your day?"

"Don't ask," came her husband's jovial reply. This affectionate ritual would expand to his children—Blaine Junior and Teri, with his chauvinist character in full swing. It was obvious that he greatly favored the fourteen-year-old image of himself.

"Did you protect your mother and sister today when I was gone, Junior?"

"I sure did, Dad!"

"I'm proud of you, boy!"

His thirteen-year-old-daughter, who was a young clone of her mother, was not so fortunate. "Did you help your mother today, Teri?"

"Yes, I did, Father."

The man of the house was about to have his long day extended. It was music to his ears however, when his wife told him that she accepted a barbecue invitation from Gary Harris.

"Finally, some people who make sense!" was Blaine's reaction as he raised his arms in approval.

That evening the two families gathered around a fire pit, where the dads, moms, brothers and sisters paired up. Throughout the evening, Blaine would discreetly look at his friend and say, "I'll settle everything tomorrow after church."

Gary would assure his friend that everything was okay between them.

***

Blaine tossed and turned all night long over the bumps and bruises he encountered that day. Worst of all was the agony of being willing to borrow any amount from his best friend and having to wait an entire day to resolve it. Finally, he awoke, knowing that he was approaching the hour where he could return the dollar he borrowed and resume his life. As luck would have it, the impatient rancher got ahead of himself and went to Gary's house wearing the shirt he wore in church. The bill was still in the pen pocket of the shirt he had worn the day before.

Strike one.

"I can't believe this!" exclaimed Blaine as he laughed at himself. Give me a few minutes and I'll be back."

"You don't need to give it back to me," said his friend. "Just keep it."

That comment made Blaine feel a bit befuddled, with his pride getting stirred. "I can't do that," he explained. "It might be small, but I did make a deal with you."

Gary seemed to pass off the entire situation as being petty and said, "I was just leaving. We can handle this later."

"Sure," replied Blaine as they shook hands. His anxiety was reaching new heights as he watched his friend leave his home and drive off in his pickup. Immediately, he went home and changed into a shirt that would always carry the dollar he owed.

It was later that Sunday when the Wolf family went to town to have lunch and take a walk in a local park. It was there when the rumor mill fired its second salvo. Sheriff Chesterfield and his wife for over forty years, Daisy, crossed paths with the family.

***

Sheriff Merle Emerson Chesterfield was once a fierce law- man who slowed down many moons ago. Today he was just a figurehead with a badge, but unlike the town's mayor- he knew it. The old codger who was born in the hills was fully aware that he and his wife were being looked after in a town where everybody knew everyone. That, along with the godsend of having enough sensible adults to control things, allowed him to get away with just going through the motions and looking the part.

Merle did just that; from the top of his white ten-gallon hat to the silver tips on his boots. The gray, lanky figure who walked with a limp, looked like something from an old western movie. One that included the traditional vest, handlebar mustache and the slight whistle when he talked.

Quick-witted and always willing to help, the harmless sixty-four-year-old was certainly in the right town to finish out his career.

***

"Blaine Wolf!" cried out the man nearing retirement. "How are

30

you and your family doing this fine Sunday?"

It was always a pleasure to watch Sheriff Chesterfield and his wife hold hands. "We're all doing just fine, Sheriff. It's so nice to see you two," responded Blaine.

The elected official initiated action to address a situation where he felt he could make a difference. Placing an arm around Blaine's neck, he corralled the muscle-bound cattleman and guided him away saying, "Hey, let's have a little talk."

This approach caught the rancher by surprise. Still, Blaine respected the goodhearted sheriff and cooperated. Daisy apparently knew what her husband was up to and initiated a conversation while leading the others in another direction.

Once out of view, Merle Chesterfield stopped the big man and placed a hand on each of his broad shoulders. "Ya know," he said, "I'm one of many who has a lot of respect for you, Blaine."

"Well, I appreciate that," said Blaine. Leaning forward, he asked in a polite tone, "Can you tell me what this is about?"

The sheriff looked at the family man with steel-blue eyes and said, "Look, Blaine, we all know how hard things are nowadays, and the Chesterfields just want to help a little bit for those who still have children to raise. It's absolutely nothing about you personally," he said. The old-timer then placed a small wad of rolled-up cash in Blaine's oversized hand and winked at him.

"Sheriff Chesterfield, you don't need to do this for us," Blaine said in a grateful tone.

"It's all right," he said, placing a hand on Blaine's shoulder. "Don't you think the missus and I are fully aware of what you and the other men in this town do for us? We know that I would have been voted out of long ago if you didn't back us the way you do."

Blaine looked down at his feet like a child caught lying and said, "Well..."

Merle slapped him on the shoulder and said, "Just accept it; you have no idea how happy this will make us."

Blaine understood that the couple who never had children of their own occasionally made an effort to somehow gift a family in the area. Through that understanding, the proud native accepted the monetary gift.

It was then when Sheriff Merle Chesterfield gave additional information that made Blaine do a double take. Leaning to his ear as if to tell a secret, he whispered, "Most people don't know about this, but in Goldenview, they have a food bank with free clothing-where they don't ask any questions." The concerned sheriff delivered what he had to say. He gave Blaine a friendly elbow to

31

the midsection and then tipped his hat with a radiant smile as big as the sun and returned to his wife.

It was one of the most peculiar moments Blaine had ever experienced. He was holding money he didn't earn and was just tipped off about a well-supplied food bank in a neighboring town. *What is he talking about?* He thought. At that moment, he began to place the donation into his pen pocket, where his question was answered. Gary's bill was neatly folded and tucked inside, obstructing the cash he was trying to conceal.

Immediately, it dawned on him that word about him borrowing a dollar must have spread further. *They must think we're poor!* he concluded while shaking his head with embarrassment. The day in town was officially aborted with the man of the house announcing, "I want to get out of here!"

That evening at the dinner table, one Blaine Wolf was talking under his breath in frustration. His wife and children knew this side of his character and were fully aware that it was best not to ask anything. The supportive wife massaged her husband's shoulders before serving dinner. The entree presented began to lift his spirits. To his surprise, it was something different that brought with it a tantalizing aroma. Placed in the center of the table was a hearty casserole in a porcelain container he didn't recognize. The warm meal was so good that Blaine had seconds. Once the deep dish was scraped clean, he just had to pay the chef a compliment. "Where did you learn to cook like that?" he asked.

"It wasn't me," replied the good wife. "Someone left it on our porch today with this envelope addressed to our family." The conscientious woman knew who wore the pants in the family and had saved it for her husband.

Stacey handed it to him, where he promptly opened it and pulled out an inspiring card with a picture of a sunrise over a mountain range. Written inside was a message of hope and encouragement in beautiful handwriting. It also reminded the household that the community was strong and would gladly help them through hard times. Last, it was requested to leave the container on their porch, and they would drop by later to discreetly take it back home.

The envelope still had some weight to it. Reaching inside, he pulled out pamphlets that offered a multitude of social services that included their 1-800 numbers. It was then when Blaine realized that Judge Alvin's informal sentence had drawn the wrong attention to his life. White-knuckled and full of anger, he frightened his entire family by crying out, **"What!"**

That evening, Blaine personally washed the eloquent cookware and placed it on his front porch. From there, he spent the rest of the evening peering through a corner of the closed drapes in his living room...

7

Monday came, with Judge Alvin finishing a late breakfast at the Bee Hive Cafe. With him, sat an opportunistic Mayor Marcus Hipple who hungered for a more desirable image. To see the elected officials together in public was definitely a pairing that personified an odd couple in epic proportions. Alvin was fine with that. His only concern was a person's heart—not their last name.

That morning, Alvin had a battle on two fronts:

1. Marcus Hipple was again, trying too hard to fit in.

2. The write-in mayor arrived that day, having made two modifications to enhance his outwardly appearance. First of all, he showed up wearing a pair of Bermuda shorts that survived years in the local thrift store—apparel that complimented his white socks and sandals personally selected for warmer climates.

Secondly, he just applied his first coat of the latest men's hair dye as seen on TV, and was proud as a peacock! True, heads turned everywhere he went that morning. An understanding Alvin upheld the mayor's dignity and willfully shared his morning for all to see.

It was at that moment when a frustrated Blaine Wolf entered the diner. The man, who earlier missed the friend he owed money to, was further upset that the casserole dish used for bait was retrieved while he got a glass of water. It would be an understatement to say that Blaine Harold Wolf could use some cheering up. Upon seeing the hand that life had dealt Alvin, a devious smile gradually crossed his face. Quietly, he sat within earshot of their table without Marcus being aware. Alvin was cool and gave a slight nod to the rancher as a way to promise that he wouldn't blow his cover. Starving for food and something to smile about, the anxiety-ridden local ordered steak and eggs and watched the show.

"Hey, don't you like to fish?" asked Marcus, using a tone meant to attract others.

"No, I don't like to fish," responded Alvin.

Marcus sat back in disbelief, having heard many fishing stories that evolved around trips with the beloved judge. "I love to fish!" he said, giving a thumbs-up. Marcus was relieved to hear that.

Blaine nodded his head in approval as to where the conversation was going. In a split second, Alvin winked back as Marcus reached for his coffee.

"Can I share a secret with you?" asked the mayor in a lower voice.

"Sure," answered Alvin.

Leaning forward, the balding man with patches of shiny hair made a confession. "I have never gone fishing before, but always wanted to."

Blaine looked up, shaking his head out of pity. "That's a crime," said Alvin with a dash of humor. Blaine could only agree and nodded his head profusely.

What happened next was testimony to the love and goodwill that was Alvin Hershel Wong's signature. "Ya know what?" he asked.

"What?" replied Marcus in a nervous tone.

Using two fingers, he gave the mayor a slight tap on his chest and said, "You and I need to get out there for a night and do it!"

Marcus was momentarily at a loss for words and leaned back with his mouth wide open. With the exception of the townsfolk gathering around him when he was appointed mayor, he was never sought out for anything. Normally, he had to crash the party when dropping hints didn't work. "You mean, you and me fishing?" he asked.

"And camping," added Alvin.

Marcus Hipple clenched a fist and dropped it on the table while looking up. All he could say was, *"Wow."*

Alvin began to mix in a bit of his humor, only to have it unveil a red flag. "I hope you aren't one of those guys who has a Pocket Fisherman..."

That comment perked up the adult nerd. He got close to Alvin's face and pointed out a significant fact: "You gotta admit that the man on those commercials caught a lot of fish with one!"

Blaine was following the conversation and involuntarily spat out a piece of steak.

Alvin made a snide remark under his breath. "I suppose if I got a stick with some string, and stuck a worm on a safety pin- and then rented a fish hatchery for an hour; I'd probably..."

"What?" asked a confused Marcus, not understanding what was being said.

"Nothing," said Alvin. "Never mind..."

"It's still in its plastic package, fresh as new!" boasted Marcus.

Alvin saw Blaine slap his hand on the table in silent laughter. It was apparent that the mayor had painted a visual that Blaine could envision.

"Wood! We'll need wood!" exclaimed the man with soft hands and well-manicured fingernails. "I can get packages of it at the store," said Marcus.

"Have you ever heard of an axe?" asked Alvin with a touch of scrutiny. "Tell you what," he continued. "You and I will keep in touch, and I'll let you know when the time is right."

"Do you want to make out a list of things I need to bring?" asked Marcus.

"No," replied Judge Alvin. "In fact, don't bring a thing. I'll take care of the rest."

The topic came to an end with Mayor Hipple finally excusing himself from the table. He left a reasonable tip, paid his bill and left.

At that point, Blaine's breakfast was reduced to a final cup of coffee as he sat down where Marcus was. "Are you crazy?" he asked Alvin. "Are you actually going to spend a night with him in the middle of the woods?"

"I sure am," came the reply. "There's nothing wrong with that guy."

"Did you get a load of his outfit today and what he did to his hair?" the big man said with a chuckle.

"Yes, I did," said Alvin. "Just remind me to shoot myself if I ever begin to do something like that." Both men laughed mildly. "All kidding aside, he's just like you and me; he's a caring, harmless person who's trying his best."

Blaine became a bit reserved and did what he could to show some respect to their mayor. "Yeah, I guess he's okay…"

Alvin then pushed a button that went against the grain. "We can include Gavin Woodley on that list too."

Blaine didn't see that remark coming and took it as an attack. From there, a knee-jerk response fired out like a cannonball. "I was just trying to teach that boy a lesson!"

"You're calling a thirty-two-year-old guy with a family a boy?" Alvin said with a wince.

"I was just trying to teach him a lesson!" yelled the employer. Hastily, he fumbled for change out of his pocket and left it on the table. Without saying a word, he left to pay his bill and stormed out of the diner, mad at the entire world.

The day was still new, with his kids in school and his wife out with Penny Harris. Wisely the man with a short temper chose to return home and blow off steam—a move that would inadvertently continue his downward spiral where fate awaited...

8

———— •••• ————

It would be an endless task to list the many pet peeves that were known to get under the skin of Blaine Harold Wolf. One of whom was a door-to-door salesman who in his eyes, *was a desperate, opportunistic, failing entrepreneur who was down to his last gimmick. A trespasser who intentionally took advantage of the Stacey Wolfs of the world, knowing that their hardworking husbands were away supporting their families.*

The miffed rancher was in the comforts of his own home when there was a knock at the front door. His eyes dilated in hopes that it was his neighbor, Gary, who would tip the scales even on their pact. The cure that would subside any speculation about his welfare and allow him to continue his life. Playing the odds, Blaine removed the dollar from his shirt pocket and merrily opened the door while waving the greenback high in the air.

To his surprise, he was confronted by a well-dressed African American male in his prime.

The paper money went quickly back into his pen pocket, with his expression turning from day to night. Sarcastically, he looked for a vacuum cleaner he assumed was to be peddled. There wasn't one in sight, but the charming man did hold a thin leather briefcase. "Isn't that kinda small to be selling brushes?" asked the homeowner.

"Sir," replied the stranger, who enunciated in proper English. "I'm not here to sell you brushes."

Before the polite man could continue, Blaine interrupted with authority, "Well, if it's life insurance, I'm already taken care of..."

The lean man who stood even with Blaine, saw humor in what was said and laughed as he spoke. "No, I'm not here as a life insurance salesman either."

Blaine's curiosity was piqued as he stopped guessing. "Then what brings you here?"

"Mr. Wolf, my name is Steven Hayes, and I'm here on behalf of the County Family Assistance Program. It has been brought to our attention that you may qualify for a…"

"I don't want any!" yelled the defensive taxpayer as he rudely slammed the door in the social worker's face and locked it.

The irate provider spent the rest of his afternoon throwing a tantrum while pacing throughout the house. Gradually, he began to calm down when his children came home carrying their books and lunches. "Weren't you hungry today?" asked the dad.

Teri was bright-eyed and answered quickly. "Everyone in school was nice to us today. We were given so much food that we couldn't eat what Mom made!"

"They even filled our lunch bags so that we could take some home!" Junior added.

Blaine slapped his hand across his forehead and went to his room to digest it all.

In a short time, his wife came home and went straight to the bedroom. Holding a cardboard box with both hands she announced, "I'm certainly liking this town more and more!"

"What's in the box?" he asked.

"Seems to be all sorts of things," she said. "Clothing, frozen dinners, candles- a lot of things."

"You don't know what you bought today?" he asked.

"I didn't buy anything today. Penny and I decided to drop by the Women's Club, and they greeted me as if I were royalty. They asked me how our family was doing and presented me with this box that had my name written on it. Wasn't that thoughtful?" she commented unassumingly.

Blaine went to the bathroom muttering and locked himself in.

***

That evening was to be Blaine's night out with the guys to go bowling. Initially, he wanted to write off the day as a loss, but his wife talked him into going. "It will do you good to get out with your friends," she pointed out. Blaine thought about it and realized that as usual, she was right. He commented that he did want to meet up with Gary anyway. "Oh, I forgot to tell you," she said. "Penny told me that her husband had to leave town for a while to help his brother build a barn."

"Oh great," commented a dejected Blaine as he threw up his hands.

"Is there something wrong?" she asked. Blaine always kept his affairs private from everyone, including his wife. "No, everything's okay..." came his reply.

That night, Gary's absence had Blaine reassigned to team up with Billy Turner—the area's top bowler.

***

Billy Turner was a highly decorated retired military man who was heavily involved with youth groups. The African American rendition of Blaine Wolf 's stature was blessed with a more even keel and better discretion when dealing with others. Not one to be judgmental, he always had a smile and openly cared for others. The man was happily married with a cavalcade of children and grandchildren to boot.

On more than one occasion, he was asked to tour on the professional level.

***

The team Blaine advanced to was clearly the pick of the litter. It consisted of Billy, his fifty-year-old cousin, Phillip, Alvin Wong and himself: all substantial bowlers—if not better. This grouping spelled out success, with Blaine starting to enjoy his life a little better.

"Hey, Wolf," Billy called out. "I've been asked to try a hand lotion that claims that with this stuff; you don't need to put your fingers into any holes—just palm it. Do you want to try some?"

"I appreciate the offer, but I'm going to pass," replied Blaine. The others were willing to try this experiment as Blaine got ready to bowl first. His first shot was a flop and ended in the gutter. "Did I do that?" Blaine cried out as he apologized to his team.

"Don't worry about it, Wolf," said Billy as he patted him on the back. "We know you're good, and we have a whole game ahead of us."

Embarrassed that he put his side in the hole, Blaine stood back and quietly watched Billy throw his ball. The experimental lotion did not live up to its promise and sent Billy's ball following in the same path as Blaine's. After Phillip and Alvin had the same results, the trio realized that they needed to wash their hands and then get down to business.

Blaine had a different perception of things and related their play to the enormous amount of charity that his supposedly destitute family had been receiving lately. Forgetting that the lotion, not their heart, was the culprit behind their performance, he decided that he

40

had enough and blew his cork.

At the top of his lungs, he blew a hurricane and addressed Billy first. "You don't think that I know what's going on around here?" he shouted.

"Blaine, what's up with you?" questioned Billy.

"It's like that casserole my family had for dinner the other night," the accuser cried out. "Well, let me tell you, mister- it was very good. In fact, I had seconds! Does that make you feel any better?"

Billy and the others knew nothing about the casserole that was left on his porch. "Well, just as long as you liked it..." Billy commented in a nonthreatening tone.

The next victim was Phillip as Blaine blasted his paranoia full-force in his face. "And about that friend of yours, Mr. Hayes..."

Phillip Turner didn't know anyone by the last name of *Hayes*, but realized that it was apparent that Blaine did.

"You can tell him to go provide services for other families- but not mine!" expressed the volatile teammate.

"Okay; whatever you say, brother Blaine," came Phillip's soft response.

Alvin was last on the pecking order. "We don't need to have your children feeding my children in school!" he yelled.

Alvin looked up to him with his innocent brown eyes and said, "I don't have any kids. I've never been married before—honest!"

Standing back, he looked around at the many eyes that were looking back and yelled his final statement. "I know you're all in on this!" On that note, he stormed out to the parking lot.

Blaine was in no shape to return home and thought that a good traditional American hamburger and shake would calm him down. Hangman had one such drive-in, and it was there that he would dine. A half hour later Blaine was inside Willard's Burgers finishing up his Deluxe Basket. It was when he was leaving the establishment where a group of youth approached him. One adolescent boy took notice at the shoes he was wearing and pointed at them. "Cool, man! Hey, mister; where did you get those?"

Blaine looked down and saw the red, beige and green shoes, with red laces, that caught his attention. At that moment, it dawned on him that his cowboy boots were left behind at the bowling alley. Turning around, the group saw an additional feature: The number 13 was centered on the back of each heel.

"Wow, check that out!" another cried out.

It was then when Blaine saw the town gossip, Mrs. Driscoll, observe the interaction with a look of disappointment on her face.

Naturally, she had to put in her two cents: "Aren't you kinda old to be hanging out with them, Blaine?" The rancher was confused, embarrassed and upset. He remained quiet and then frantically left for his truck. His frustrations had him hit the accelerator violently while rolling through a mud puddle, causing the tires to burn rubber on the dry pavement. The teens were further impressed and wanted to know more about this guy!

Mrs. Driscoll saw it all and took notes.

9

Blaine Wolf's family was accustomed to seeing him come home fit to be tied. In such instances, they allowed him his space and waited until the next day to address him. The following morning started with Blaine finding his boots on his front steps. They reminded him of the disastrous evening he had the night before.

"What you need to do is to get away for a day," his loving wife suggested the following morning.

"Yeah, I guess you're right," he calmly agreed. At that moment, his conscience began to kick in and realized that lately he had been a bit rough on his nephew, Grant. "I suppose I could take Grant with me as a way to brighten up his day a bit."

"Oh, he would love that!" exclaimed Stacey as she kissed her husband on the cheek.

Within an hour the two were driving off to an unknown adventure. Before leaving, the elder had outlined a pact he demanded the young man to follow. *"I promise I will not to talk to strangers anymore,"* vowed Grant.

Their first stop was at the bowling alley, where Blaine discreetly left something in a brown paper bag. "What are you doing?" asked the puzzled nephew.

"Oh, nothing..." he replied.

Off and running, the odd couple decided to have a hearty breakfast just out of town. It was there where Blaine found the opportunity he was waiting for. In the parking lot was the distinct red pickup of none other than Gary Harris himself!

"Praise the Lord!" he cried out while pounding on the steering wheel. Without any hesitation, he pulled into the empty parking stall next to it and marched into the diner.

To his delight, he immediately saw the brother team of Sam and Gary Harris and approached them. "So there you are!" exclaimed the debtor in a jolly tone as he pointed a finger at Gary.

Comically, Gary held his hands up high in the air, pleading,

"Don't shoot!" All laughed, including Grant as he stood back and remained closed-mouthed.

Blaine changed subjects. "I thought you guys were building a barn at Sam's place."

"We were, until someone forgot to bring a jack," replied Sam, looking at his sibling.

Gary sat up straight and rolled his eyes as if he was a dunce sitting in the corner.

"I could have gotten it for you," offered Blaine.

"I decided to get it myself and see what else I might have left behind," answered Gary in a humorous tone.

"Well, anyway, I've got something for you," said Blaine as he reached into his empty pen pocket. Upon touch, a devastating facial expression overcame the man's face. At that moment, he remembered that he washed his shirts the night before. The dollar that was burning a hole in his life was right where he last left it: on top of the washing machine.

Gary could tell that Blaine had misplaced the bill and said, "You can keep it. It really doesn't matter."

To Blaine Harold Wolf, it most certainly did as he balked at the idea.

"Blaine, it's only a buck," reasoned his friend.

"I have four quarters for video games," offered Grant. The uncle turned to his nephew with a stern look that immediately reminded him of the conditions set for their outing. The companion had quick recall and tightly closed his mouth.

Blaine's stubborn side was starting to blossom like that of a child determined to get his way. The dollar he was sentenced to borrow had to be the *very one* he would pay back. "I'll catch up with ya when you're back home," he told Gary.

"Sure," agreed Gary. "There's no hurry on it."

The brothers had just finished their meal and got up to leave. "Nice seeing you two," said Sam as he shook hands with Blaine and his nephew. Gary followed suit, with the brothers leaving a tip, paying the cashier and leaving. Feeling dejected, Blaine took the defeat on the chin and found a table.

Soon they finished eating and were on the highway, with Blaine's edgy side taking over. Subconsciously searching, it didn't take him long to find something to vent about. "Oh, great; a woman driver!"

"You mean that car ahead of us?" asked Grant.

"That's the one," replied his uncle.

Grant squinted for a brief moment to study the four-door sedan.

"How can you tell that the driver is a woman?" he questioned.

"Haven't you been watching her?" he asked.

"Not really," said Grant.

"Well, if you'd pay more attention, you would have noticed how she changed lanes," scolded the uncle.

"Whenever a car uses signal indicators, that's a sign right there!"

Grant was confused and didn't understand why the usage of that precautionary measure would be anything to complain about.

The Archie Bunker of Hangman had more to say. "They're the same ones who drive within the speed limit and make a full stop at every stop sign. When one of them is not sure about directions, they never challenge it on their own; instead, they pull over to get help. They should never be allowed on the road," he concluded under his breath.

Grant knew this side of his uncle's character and rolled with it. Eventually, small talk ranging from politics to childhood memories kept an even temperament until Blaine came up with an idea. "Aren't we headed towards that new mall that's supposed to have everything?" he asked.

Grant loved modern shops and knew that the mall his uncle was referring to had the latest and the newest. "You mean the Galaxy Mall?" he asked with excitement. "That's just up ahead."

"Well, we gotta find something to do; so it might as well be that," said the uncle.

"Cool!" agreed Grant as he started to fidget with anticipation. To leave a town initially settled by covered wagons and arrive at an Emerald City- was overwhelming to say the least. The futuristic shopping center came into view miles away. In time, they entered a paved sea of vehicles with one-way lanes going in all directions. "I've never seen so many cars in my entire life!" said the cattleman who was almost in shock. Safely parked, they hiked to the main entrance realizing that in no time at all, they could be separated. "How about you and I go our separate ways and meet right here at noon—then we'll get lunch somewhere?" Blaine suggested.

"Cool," came the response of his non-western nephew. The young man turned around and disappeared in the crowd.

***

When in a store, it's always wise to never wander off too far and to avoid talking to strangers. Sound advice that one Blaine Harold Wolf should have been following- as fate lurked around the corner with his name on it...

***

Blaine browsed around fascinated by the bright lights, ever-changing music and masses that represented every walk of life. It tickled him to stick his head into shops where young clerks wore multicolored hairstyles and sold trendy items he'd never seen before. He was like a lost boy wandering around in the big city, being too captivated to be aware of any possible threat. Floundering about and not knowing exactly where to go, he suddenly heard the pleasant voice of someone who was obviously addressing him.

"Excuse me, sir. I'd like to introduce myself."

Startled, he turned around only to be pleasantly surprised. There, standing before him, was a seemingly mild- mannered middle-aged man who appeared as if he was in the medical profession. The compassionate face with short dark hair conservatively parted off to the side, wore the type of glasses doctors were known to wear. His pressed, white outfit was only missing a stethoscope.

Blaine extended his massive, calloused hand and introduced himself. "Blaine Wolf." Then he added, "And you're Dr..."

The stranger immediately laughed as their hands met. "Just call me, 'Greg'; and pleased to meet you, Blaine. I bet you're probably a descendant of the settlers who built this country," he said to the man with a tanned, weathered face wearing western duds.

"I'm one of them!" Blaine replied with an air of pride. If Greg sold cars, Blaine would already be out on a test drive. The small-town resident loved what he heard and wanted more. The conversation escalated rapidly with his ego being nourished further and further. After many pats on the shoulder, Greg made his move. Taking a step back, he folded his arms and looked head to toe at his would-be client. Shaking his head in awe, he drove in the final stake: "Well, you certainly live up to your billing"

Blaine was his.

It was at that moment when Greg pulled the trigger and made an offer. "There's a reason why my staff and I picked you out in particular."

The line worked like a charm, as Blaine's expression lit up like a lottery winner. "There is?"

"Definitely," he replied. "We are in the business of taking a hardworking American like you and relaxing their tired muscles to a state as to where they can properly realign to begin the process of restoring youth and vitality."

Blaine absorbed what was said and to Gary's delight, expressed

46

interest. "Wow! How about that…"

The salesman continued.

"At least once a day, I reward my employees by having them hand-pick a deserving person, such as yourself, and administer our services for free. This automatically guarantees that we at least have reached out to the right person as a reward for what their life has meant to our society, which, in-turn- makes us feel better."

Gary elaborated further to the man with a high school diploma by maintaining his smooth-running social skills. On occasion, a medical term would be utilized at the right time. The word *free* kept running across Blaine's mind as his eyes scanned the many awkwardly dressed and accessorized individuals walking about— ones who undoubtedly had never heard of the town of *Hangman*. It seemed that Gary was the only one in the mall that the newcomer could identify with. Having ample time on his hands and feeling like the hick he often was, Blaine decided to take the entrepreneur up on his offer. A decision that would at least introduce him to something that appeared to be of some value, while being separated from the other shoppers.

It turned out that Gary was a successful chiropractor whose practice also included a licensed beautician, manicurist, pedicurist and masseuse. His office however, was nothing more than a rented space in the middle of the mall. Regardless, the quarters were neat, tidy and fitted with a friendly staff who greeted the rancher with open arms. Furthermore, they informed him that he was noticed the moment he entered the mall, *like most people did.* Moderately confined within the protection of high black velvet curtains, he was escorted inside where a black leather reclining chair and matching examination table awaited. Blaine looked around the strange environment and started to feel a bit apprehensive. Realizing that he was already committed, he continued to cooperate. At their request, he removed his hat and boots and soon lay face down on the elevated medical table.

It was there where Gary started off as lead batter. Strategically, he applied the proper amount of pressure on the knotted-up muscle tissue and massaged miracles, using a utensil to pop key bones back to their natural setting. Over and over again, he calmly told the forty-one-year-old to relax. "Just relax, Blaine. Relax."

Blaine did just that; the tired stockman buried his head into a fluffy pillow, relishing the treatment. The comfort was so great that the patient wanted to drift off into a deep sleep and forget about all of his troubles.

"You are a fantastic customer," commented Gary.

The big man could only grumble in pleasure and give a slight nod. "My staff and I are not booked today and would like to extend your free trial. Do you mind if we give you our ultimate package and use you as a model for others to see our procedure?" Blaine was about to nod off and gave the same response.

Things changed immediately when the upgrade advanced him to the recliner on wheels. Almost asleep, he was assisted to the padded chair, where his socks were removed and then a vigorous foot massage was underway. Leaning back, he stretched like a purring cat drifting off into la-la land...

Blaine began to snore, with his bass-like mouth fully inhaling and exhaling. Soon his face was being rubbed as a preparation for the coat of mud and cucumber slices that would follow. All ten nails were being filed as the westerner twisted and turned in ecstasy.

Without warning, the out-of-place prairie dweller sneezed abruptly and burped at the same time, waking himself up. Momentarily, he forgot where he was and briefly panicked upon the realization that his vision was blinded by a moist substance.

Grabbing the sliced vegetables with each hand, he sat up straight to adjust his eyes to the bright lights. In a state of confusion, he remained motionless until his vision was restored.

It was there where he encountered the most embarrassing moment of his entire life. Facing him, with astounded expressions of disbelief, was the senior section of his home-town. The group that chartered a bus to seek out adventure that day definitely got more than what they bargained for! Blaine's mouth was wide open as he leaned forward, recognizing each neighbor. The very ones who represented committees of goodwill and other charitable organizations were all present. Reality set in, putting him on the defense. Looking at Sheriff Chesterfield, he saw the look of a disappointed father. One that felt shame because of a son who spent all his money on a worthless jalopy, just because it had chrome-plated wheels. Blaine extended his hands and began to plead. "Merle, it's not what you think!"

The poker-faced lawman remained quiet, realizing that the man with the mud-coated face was, indeed, Blaine Wolf. Mrs. Driscoll stood next to him and broke the ice by asking, "Have you been doing drugs lately?" Blaine was at a loss for words, having never been accused of such a deviant act before. Surveying the many who stood before him, he felt like an innocent man on trial who was about to be put away for life. His neighbors departed for their bus, with Mrs. Driscoll having a story for the whole town.

Blaine stood up to turn around and caught his reflection in a mirror. What he saw scared the wits out of him because he had not been aware of what Gary's staff had done, and he realizing what his neighbors saw.

Losing control, he yelled, "I want to get out of here!" Grabbing a towel, he wiped most of the mud off of his face, put on his hat and boots, and left fully dressed.

It was a mixed blessing for Blaine to run into his nephew. "What's that stuff on your face?" he asked.

"None of your beeswax!" blasted the irate uncle. Grant's recall from many therapy sessions had him force a laugh on himself.

The elder countered by giving a command: "And stop doing that!"

Blaine Wolf was now the "Ted Baxter" of the valley.

The confused rancher was at a loss, not knowing where to go. On one hand, he could speed away vowing to never return to the modern complex where he made a fool out of himself. On the other, he was too embarrassed to show his face around the town he called home.

10

---•●•---

The next day found a recovering Blaine Wolf licking his wounds from his recent escapade. Luckily, he had the seclusion of his ranch where he could heal. Also, there was a multitude of chores piled up that needed attention. *I could sure use Gavin today,* he thought.

With his wife and children at school, he would visit a sacred site on the lower forty—a fenced-in area that had the name Wolf etched on every stone. One by one, he placed specially picked flowers on each grave until he reached the last marker. This was where his mother lay with a suitable array of blossoms and petals being saved for last. From there, a few prayers, along with a tear was delivered as a lone yellow butterfly landed on a petal. Finally, it came time for the cattleman to walk away and inspect his livestock.

It was a long, arduous morning under the hot sun as lunchtime approached. Hungry and feeling depressed, Blaine thought he'd go to town and have his midday meal. Once on the main street, it became obvious that there had been some talk about the misunderstood rancher. Wherever he went, he was either avoided or spoken to in an overly kind fashion from distant acquaintances.

Feeling marked, he went for a sure thing. He decided to dine at the delicatessen in Ric Bratton's store, where a true friendship was always guaranteed. Upon entering the frontier general store, a much-anticipated and much-needed greeting took place.

"Well, howdy, stranger!" Ric cried out.

"Good to see you, fella!" returned Blaine. "I bet you've heard my name mentioned a few times."

"Just a few," his friend commented. "You can relax, though. You're light-years away from reaching my level on the rumor mill," he laughed. "Remember, you're talking to a guy whose family was once accused of being communist during the McCarthy Era!"

Blaine slapped his hand on the counter, saying, "I remember hearing about that."

A few customers came and went, with some acknowledging the

popular rancher and others pretending not to see him. "It'll get better in time," Ric assured him.

"It can be hard in the meantime," said Blaine.

The customary "coffee on the house" continued to fill Blaine's cup as he placed his order. "I'll have a Ruben Sandwich with plenty of mayo—and throw in some of that potato salad you're famous for!"

"Wow, that sounds good!" replied Ric. Soon the childhood friends were sharing lunch the way they did back in grammar school. Humorous playground stories were exchanged, with summer fishing tales filling in the gaps. Ric knew the age-old cure about applying laughter to a loved one's pain and was a master at it.

Blaine had to ask an obvious question: "How do you do that?"

"Do what?" responded Ric.

"You always turn a bad situation into a happy moment," Blaine pointed out.

Ric leaned forward and spoke softly. "Can I let you in on a little secret?"

Blaine lost all expression and answered, "Sure."

"Saying a little prayer never hurts," advised Ric as he patted his friend on the back.

Ric left to serve a customer, and Blaine leaned back in the chair pondering on the words he had heard throughout his entire life.

A few bites later, the school chum left his tab on the table while waving at his friend behind the cash register. From there, Blaine went about his day mulling over the words his friend shared. Finally, he dropped what he was doing and tried something different.

He nonchalantly parked a block away from the Hangman Fellowship Church and entered its main doors when no one was watching.

***

For one Blaine Harold Wolf, the ambiance of this landmark, where families started and last sacraments were given, just about equaled that of the courthouse across the street. They were built the same year, out of the same material and by the same people.

The only difference was that this was a sanctuary with stained-glass windows. It also utilized an altar with a magnificent cross and an old pipe organ off to the side. Rituals were also followed as to when someone should kneel, stand, sit, sing or quote verses.

Blaine knew that the other was a structure incorporated when greed and misunderstandings got out of hand.

He viewed the landmarks that faced each other similar in one aspect—and opposite in another. It seemed that the courthouse would try to take someone's money through lawsuits while the church would tax its parishioners to assure them a passage to God's kingdom.

Or so he thought...

Regardless, the rancher did believe in God and respectfully removed his hat upon entering. Slowly, he walked toward the front of the empty church and sat in a middle pew. While he was getting comfortable, Pastor Johnathan Smith came out of nowhere and approached him.

***

Pastor Johnathan Joseph Smith was a dyed-in-the-wool man of faith, who followed the footsteps of practically every man in his family. Always one to accept anyone and everyone on life's terms, the man of the cloth was known for approaching those in pain and listening to them. His thin, nonthreatening presence graced the robe he wore while fine gray hair accented soulful eyes that spelled out love to anyone in need. Rosy cheeks and an eternal smile told the world that he was there to spread the Word of God.

***

"Good to see you here, brother Blaine," he called out.

Blaine was startled and almost jumped out of his seat. "Oh, you scared me!" he said, catching his breath.

The pastor joined in with the laughter and said, "Forgive me. Next time, I'll let you see me coming." The holy man squinted his eyes in deep concentration as he looked up, holding his chin. "Now let's see...Today is not Christmas, it's not Easter—nor is it Thanksgiving. I also don't recall anyone getting married today, and I hope there isn't a funeral. So tell me, Blaine, what brought you here?"

The rancher squirmed with a guilt-ridden face, knowing that he did not attend church regularly. "I'm trying to sort some things out and realized that I need some extra help," he answered.

Placing each hand on the set of broad shoulders that faced him, the pastor gazed intensely at Blaine and said, "Well, good. That's why we're here."

A warm conversation ensued, with Blaine stumbling, trying to

52

find the right words to express his feelings. "Well, you sound human to me," Pastor John encouraged as he motioned to hear more. "We're all misunderstood at times, but the Lord knows who we are," he would say.

Finally, the church leader exposed some personal flaws of his own as a way to illustrate that he was just as human. *"You mean a guy like you has marital problems?"* the rancher asked in a high-pitched voice.

"I'm on my second marriage," confessed Pastor John.

"I sometimes wonder why Stacey hadn't left me long ago," countered Blaine as he lowered his head.

Embarrassing secrets were shared with each man gaining more respect for the other. Finally, the pastor stood up and pulled out his wallet. From there, a business card was handed to the troubled rancher. "This guy is the greatest counselor I know of. That's why myself, and a few others from this very town see him. It will be our secret."

Blaine took the card and said, "Thanks, John. I just might do that."

The dejected man was now feeling a ray of hope as he placed the card in his pocket and left.

11

---•●•---

That evening, Blaine Wolf had an even temperament at the dinner table. He even spent time looking at each child's homework assignment and watched TV with the family. All of this from what Ric and Pastor John had to say. Feeling strong, he decided that he would muster up all his courage and make an appointment with the referred counselor.

The following morning, he hugged each family member as they left for the school bus. Once alone, he pulled out the business card of Wilson Peets and dialed the number. To his delight, he was not greeted by a recorded message. Instead, it was the voice of a congenial receptionist who was able to schedule him for an appointment that very day.

***

Dr. Wilson Amos Peets was a seasoned psychiatrist who hid under the informal title of 'Counselor'. To see the man in public, one would never associate him with the many plaques and diplomas that graced his waiting room. He was too busy volunteering for youth programs, fishing, playing softball or visiting with his neighbors to be bothered with the small stuff.

The stocky country boy's medium height was further complimented with electrifying blue eyes and dashing blond hair refined to a crew cut. His approach to life of being just a regular guy always won the hearts of others.

***

Normally, Blaine Harold Wolf would never reach out for help; to him, it was only a sign of weakness. This arrangement was different however, knowing that his well-respected pastor, along with a few select unknowns, had already blazed the trail. Besides, the man felt outcast in his own community, despite his best efforts and knew that he needed to use other methods to find answers. Blaine was fully aware that he was recently functioning out of character and beginning to question everything—including himself. Out of desperation, he boldly took the plunge and found himself lying on a couch with tissues close at hand.

To his surprise, he took an immediate liking to the doctor when their introduction started off on the right foot. An honest relationship based on honor, experience and anonymity, where truth was the only rule, began to unfold.

The session began on the same tempo used when they first met. It was the bantering of small talk rounding off the edges as a way to get further acquainted.

Once in gear, it didn't take long for Blaine to feel a bit vulnerable; after all, the questions were about him. The man who prided himself to be in complete control soon felt as if he were an insect trapped in a mason jar. Furthermore, the key names he mentioned were defended by the analyst who was taking notes. Will Peets began to probe deeper by introducing large words that seldom left a lecture hall.

The therapist was now speaking another language that Blaine couldn't understand. That, along with hearing his rendition of the Gavin Woodley incident- and taking Gavin's side, had him throw his hands up in the air yelling, "I was just trying to teach him a lesson!"

Blaine got up and stormed out of the building, with the feeling that he'd been sucker-punched. *Why did I come here?* He fumed. A mixture of hurt, frustration and bewilderment consumed him as he sped off to nowhere.

Round 1 was over.

***

Blaine Wolf's day started off with him being where he normally wouldn't be. This unorthodox pattern continued when he uncharacteristically went to a local park to walk off his anger. It was there where he felt the worst betrayal of his entire life.

Off in the distance, he noticed a field trip that consisted of kids from the school his children attended. In time, he spotted his two children, along with his wife who served as a volunteer. Initially, it put a smile on his face to watch his family having fun interacting with others. The harmony of laughter and play while on a nature trip brought back fond childhood memories. His mood quickly changed however, when he noticed that his family was getting too close to certain family members he deemed *undesirable*.

These were children whose parents were migrant workers or subsidized by public assistance. To say that Blaine Wolf was proud of his heritage would be an understatement. The brash cowman also knew that everyone had heard of the Wolf name. It went without saying that he believed in a separation of classes.

The man who never allowed Halloween candy to be passed out on his property winced as he watched his son toss a ball to one of their children.

"You don't have a choice if they go to your school, but just remember you're still better than them!" their dad would preach. It caused him great pain to see his boy lower himself by fraternizing with a member from the wrong side of the tracks. Looking away, he saw his daughter committing the same act. She was paired up with another outcast she was conversing with and was sharing a can of pop. Next to her was his wife—hugging a woman whose family always knew to avoid him in public. They obviously disregarded his wishes and openly accepted these people, who had but no choice to frequent food banks and wore clothing from the thrift stores.

This picture was worth a thousand words and revealed that his family had a secret life away from him. One that was far more acceptable in society and shared happiness.

Still undetected, he lowered his head and left for home.

Once there, he walked with his dog, to the farthest point of his property and leaned against a fence. Blaine was drowning emotionally, thinking about the many people who were disappointed in him. He thought about the faces that noticed him— only to cross the street. About those who changed what they were talking about when he came into view and about the times people were *too nice* to him. He began to question whether he was just the village idiot and whether the entire town, including his family, was simply pacifying him all these years.

At least I still have, Blue, he thought while petting his dog.

At that moment, Blaine's attention was caught by a tumbleweed racing off in the distant tundra. The prairie winds were beginning to kick up, causing it to roll, bounce high and change directions in mid-flight. Suddenly, it occurred to him that he was that tumbleweed at the mercy of the violent crosswinds. It was like a cat batting a dead sparrow away from one boundary, only to change directions before reaching the other. A seemingly useless, decayed mass that no one would lay claim to like an abandoned animal or an unwanted child.

The grown man knew that it was grace that allowed him to be alone with the only friend who had ever watched him cry. The child inside broke free and sobbed in front of all creation.

***

Blaine was distant from his family that evening, using the excuse "I'm not hungry," a phrase that translated into "Leave me alone."

The breadwinner, who was now disillusioned about his own household, would seek seclusion for the rest of the night. He would dwell in the comforts of his "man cave"— the barn where family artifacts let him live in yesterday's glory. A 'mood-swing-chamber' that could only be shared with Blue.

If Blaine Wolf were a raging alcoholic, this would be the battlefront. With coffee mug in hand, he entered the massive structure that was built by his forefathers.

The descendant shuffled his feet inward through hay strands that covered the dirt floor. Once safely inside, he stopped to become one with his surroundings. Looking to the far corner, he saw an antique that, by all rights, should be in a museum. It was one of the state's first cast iron tractors that was powered by steam and was a proud statement from the Wolf family—expressing that they had adapted to the latest technology to stay even with progress.

Blaine would go farther back in time like an archeologist measuring an excavation. He looked at the family's horse- drawn plows and relic farm equipment that was designed before the industrial revolution. Modern-day tools from past eras that permitted the settlers to grow their own crops. Looking farther, he saw rusted steel blades hung on walls and accompanied with matching picks and axes—all with shiny wood handles from human sweat. There were also worn-out leather saddles, lanterns and coiled rope that hadn't been touched in decades.

Finally, he turned to the most prized possession in the Wolf family history. Enshrined alongside a distant wall was the 1853 Studebaker Brothers built wagon that carried his ancestors across much of North America. They had arrived on this *Mayflower* to start a new life.

Blaine was always captivated by the remarkably well-preserved artifact with blue-green paint and pink wheels. Throughout his life, he had wanted to put the wagon on the encrusted parallel grooves that stopped at their property- and travel the very tracks that led to the mountains and across the country. He wanted the adventure of riding the wagon back as a way to trace their family history. In school, the boy would daydream with a vivid imagination about placing a sail on the prairie schooner with the belief that it would travel faster than a train and fly over canyons.

Dwelling in his natural element with man's best friend, Blaine Wolf was momentarily at peace.

12

———•●•———

Judge Alvin started the week showing mild symptoms of spring fever. His timing couldn't have been better: his schedule was virtually free with a restrung trout pole commanding attention.

True to his word, Alvin called Mayor Marcus Stanley Hipple to make good of a promise. "Trust me," he said, "You can take a few days off. There's nothing going on around here…" Alvin remembered that his friend had never fished before and reminded him that he would bring all that was needed.

"Just dress as if you were going for a walk at night," the judge instructed.

It was agreed that Alvin would drop by the rookie's house in an hour.

Later that afternoon, the two buds were found at Eagle's Lake with lines in the water and a crackling fire. "Ahhh, this is the life!" exclaimed Alvin as he stretched out his arms.

The stage was set with a coffeepot on one corner of the grill, accompanied with a covered frying pan of wild rice and buttered bread. Folding chairs, two tents and a distinct scent of alpine made their camp the envy of the lake. The journeyman angler who elected to use a slip-sinker method to allow a marshmallow and worm dance off the lake's bottom commented, "This is how I like to fish. I let *them* come to us."

"Don't flies and lures work?" asked Marcus.

Leaning back, Alvin gave his response. "They do, but this method guarantees me a prized catch."

"Trout?" guessed Marcus.

"No," replied Alvin. "It's our friendship that I want to go home with. We'll let our poles do the work. I'd rather visit with you over a good cup of coffee. Now that's fishing!" he added while patting Marcus on the back.

The fellow bachelor with underdeveloped social skills was taken by those words. He leaned back knowing that the compliment was

59

sincere and felt a lifetime of pain being secreted from his body.

At that moment, Marcus's line grew taunt- almost jerking the pole into the lake. Instinctively, he grabbed it as Alvin exclaimed, "That's gotta be at least two pounds!" Reaching for the net, he instructed, "Just take your time and reel it in slowly."

It was sunset with one large rainbow and a six-incher grilling over the fire. Alvin winced at his companion and asked, "Are you sure you've never fished before?"

The boy who caught his first fish could only grin ear to ear. Soon, the dinner from heaven was served on paper plates with Marcus insisting that he lead in saying grace. "It makes everything complete," he pointed out.

How right he was. A prayer of thanks was given, with Alvin seeing a special side of his fishing companion that he never knew.

What was possibly the most rewarding meal they could ever imagine was credited as a gift from the Lord. It was as if God's grace allowed a timeout in life that promised a memory that would last forever. Each tender, succulent bite enhanced their faith with the realization of how fortunate they were to be alive. After dinner, Alvin stoked the fire where male bonding would ensue. From there, a brotherhood was formed with well-guarded secrets and insecurities shared.

Marcus felt comfortable enough to address the hand he was dealt in life. Looking up, he noticed the first star of the night and took a deep breath of mountain air while gathering his thoughts.

***

"Do you know what it's like to always be made fun of by people you thought were your friends?" he asked.

Alvin not only understood the question, but he could relate to it wholeheartedly. "Who do you think you're talking to?" came his reply.

Marcus was stunned by his comment and looked at him in dismay. "You're the most popular guy in town!" he exclaimed with open hands.

"We live in a small town," explained Alvin. "Everyone is popular." Marcus leaned back with his mouth wide open and digested his comment. "All of us get teased one way or another," he added. "It's just an ugly fact of life. What I get is a racist joke pointed toward other backgrounds, as if they're trying to bypass my heritage so as to not offend me. Well let me tell you, they do because I'm just as non-white as their victims are!" he said with conviction. "When you laugh at those horrible jokes, you join them in attacking anything that doesn't look like them—including me."

Marcus knew exactly what Alvin was talking about and felt ashamed. "I'm...I'm sorry, Alvin. I never realized that..."

Immediately, Alvin interrupted his friend saying, "I'm not mad at you. I'm not mad at anyone. I just wish that people could be more considerate towards others, that's all."

"I guess I really don't have anything to complain about," said Marcus in a soft voice.

"I don't see why," agreed Alvin. "That clean living you're known for has taken care of you just fine."

"I still feel that I don't quite fit in the way most people do," said Marcus.

Alvin had something to say: "You're not an embarrassment. You are a standard that prompted the township to handpick you as our mayor. If others seem a bit distant from you, it's because they're consumed with personal issues." Alvin finished the topic with an old saying that brought comfort: "Remember: you only tease the one you love."

Marcus felt good inside and wanted to continue the good therapy that came with Alvin. He would now focus on a broader topic that always eluded him: women.

"Have you ever noticed Katie Kaiser?" asked Marcus.

"Katie Kaiser?" responded Alvin in a high-pitched voice. "Every guy in town dreams about her!"

"She certainly carries herself well," commented Marcus. "That she does," agreed Alvin. "That gal's all class." Marcus paused and then spoke with a quiver of hesitation. "I always wanted to go out with her."

"It's a long line, from what I hear," replied Alvin. Marcus felt dejected and lowered his head, saying, "Yeah, I guess you're right."

"Right about what?" asked Alvin.

"Why would Katie Kaiser want to be seen with a guy like me anyway?" commented the mayor with shiny hair.

"Well, it would help if you'd just be yourself," suggested Alvin.

"Are you talking about my hair?" Marcus asked in a hush-hush voice.

"Yes," answered Alvin. "That, along with your choice of outfits and trying too hard to be liked by everyone. It pushes you backwards. Just be that regular guy who is inside you— the one who we appointed to be our mayor," said Alvin. "That's the guy everyone wants to know."

The message hit home like a ton of bricks as the mayor's face turned shades of red.

"In regards to Katie; just be yourself and ask her out for a cup of coffee," he advised.

Hope was rekindled as a starry-eyed Marcus leaned forward and asked, "Do you think she'll ever go out with me?"

"Not at first, but in time- maybe," predicted Alvin. "Just remember to be 'Marcus'; and that, my friend- will promise you your best results." An encouraging pat on the back followed with Marcus beginning to access who he really was.

13

---•●•---

Blaine Wolf awoke the next day believing that he had found the solution to his problems. He would simply close the gates to his kingdom, thus limiting entry only to family and select friends. Within his narrow mind, he concluded that this remedy would serve as a cure-all. The controversial rancher would soon learn however, that what was common practice for an ostrich- would never work for a man in Hangman.

At breakfast, the family could sense that he was up to something. The head of household was obviously preoccupied in thought. The gathering continued with pleasantries being exchanged. Toward the end of the meal, each member wished the other to have a good day.

"Oh, don't worry; I will," came the sarcastic reply. Within twenty minutes, the mother and her two children left for the bus stop with Blaine closing the massive barrier moments later. "There!" he proclaimed in victory.

His determination to isolate his world from society escalated into a frenzy. Within a day, he boldly implemented a curfew and banned his children from extracurricular activities. When asked why, he would shout: "We don't need to be out there. We have the best of everything right here!"

True, the Wolf homestead had a brook that passed through their property with a few ponds that bolstered trout of enviable size. It also had rich green pastures that rolled to viewpoints overlooking distant valleys and mountain ranges. In fact, meadows crawling with lavish foliage and colorful plants blanketed throughout this haven.

It would have been the perfect community park for Hangman, and therein lies the problem: It was the same scenario as a rich kid who had every plaything in the world- but never allowed to have friends over because of an over-protective parent. Blaine Wolf was so consumed by an image he felt denied, that he willfully went back through time to relive his family's rich history—before there was a township.

There was more. Inside his barn was a hidden crawl- space where a small metal cigar box lay. It rested in a shallow hole that allowed the container to be even with the ground. Dried hay covered the floor, hiding the antique. In its contents were many coins ranging from the 1860 era. The value of this collection could easily be exchanged for a nice car.

It wasn't their market value that held Blaine's attention though. It was the moment in 'Wolf history' that each represented. At one time or another, a fee was charged to every family in Hangman from the Wolf family.

Town history clearly states that from its origin, the Wolf settlement had unjustly claimed land that was to be shared by the township. A form of extortion that gouged a newly formed community that relied on one another.

Emergency situations that required water or permission to pass through their property to gain access to important trails often had a service charge attached. An empire controlled by the Wolf family, *or so he thought.*

Blaine spent many evenings marveling at the coins as if he were from a royal line that taxed peasants.

By Friday, his world came to a screeching halt. His wife and kids did not return home from school. Instead, he was taken by surprise by an unexpected visit from concerned relatives.

Answering a knock at the door, he found himself confronted by an angry brother, sister and in-law fit to be tied. He allowed them in as a less-than-friendly powwow was about to unfold.

"Your son wasn't at basketball practice!" screamed his older brother, Bob who assisted in coaching.

"Your wife and daughter said that they weren't allowed to attend the Girl's Club anymore!" yelled his sister, Donna who usually gave them a ride home.

A defensive Blaine Wolf fired back, demanding to know where his wife and kids were. "I took care of that," responded his sister-in-law, Bonnie. "I told them that you approved of the pizza party I was having at my house tonight and asked me to take them there after school so that they could have fun with their friends." She then got within inches of his face and said, "And they believed me."

Blaine was perplexed, realizing that he was surrounded by the family members he trusted most. The only ones who knew when to tactfully intervene when a growing problem was getting out of hand.

All done as a labor of love.

At that moment, it occurred to the big man how abusive he had been to his family, and he began to shake. "It would be nice if they could stay the night. We plan on watching some good movies with popcorn," Bonnie added.

Blaine responded in a soft voice while looking at the floor. Fighting tears, he complied by saying, "Yeah, I could at least do that for them." Looking up, he surrendered by shaking hands with each present and said, "I'll pack an overnight bag for them."

The visit was thought to be a success, with Blaine's brother putting an arm around him and whispering, "I'm so proud of you."

Blaine nodded, realizing that he needed to address personal issues. Regardless of giving in, he still wasn't certain if isolating his family from the township was such a wrong thing to do...

14

————•●•————

Saturday morning arrived with one Blaine Wolf feeling like the Lone Ranger. He awoke alone and needed a friend to confide in. Circumstances had his choices narrowed down to one person: Ric Bratton: the ideal guy to address the crossroads of where he now stood.

A quick shave and a shower was followed by a jaunt to the general store. If Blaine Wolf was suffering from severe sunburn, then Ric's "Howdy stranger!" would be the aloe vera lotion needed. In time, the two were sharing fresh coffee at a polished table in the far corner.

As always, Ric started off the bantering by laughing at himself. Small, harmless stories about how he forgot, was overlooked or misinterpreted by someone, something or somehow that resulted in a room full of laughter.

Using his one-of-a-kind brotherly love, Ric began to delude Blaine's personal insecurities by sharing war stories of his own. "I still remember when a bird flew into my windshield. Within an hour Mrs. Potter had the ASPCA pay me a visit because supposedly, it was an intentional act." Swaying his arms to the side with palms up he shrugged, adding:

"The kicker was that my car was parked in front of the post office while I was inside mailing a letter. She assumed that I must have driven quite a while with that poor sparrow on my hood..."

Slapping his knee, Blaine laughed out loud saying, "I remember that!"

From there, an occasional customer would come in and do business while Ric filled in the gaps with one humiliating story after another. At times, he would place a foot on a chair and gaze through the window while clinching his chin with one hand. Digging further, he would say, "Now let's see..." Then a hilarious incidence from his past would surface. Later, after others bought their goods and briefly visited, he would return with: "Oh, and then there was the time when…"

Blaine was in stitches with an aching stomach, but he still wanted to hear more! Eventually, things calmed down with the men comparing notes. "I'd be lost without your friendship," confided Blaine.

"I wouldn't trade you for all the gold in the world," he replied with sincerity.

"You're probably aware that I've been a goat around here lately," said Blaine.

"You might be catching up, but you'll never pass me!" quipped Ric. At that moment, he strategically channeled the conversation toward the value of seeking counseling. "I've had numerous occasions when life gave me no choice but to reach out," he admitted under his breath.

"You?" questioned Blaine with astonishment.

The silver-haired man in glasses stared directly at him and said, "Yes, me…"

Blaine sat back with a blank look as the shopkeeper got up to serve another customer. Periodically, a lull in the action would allow their conversation to continue with the curious rancher asking questions. "They are a different kind of trusted friend," Ric would answer. Finally, within the comfort of Ric Bratton's company, he asked if he could see the very one that Ric frequented. To his surprise, he was handed the business card of one Wilson Amos Peets.

In any small town, a grown man reaching out for advice and encouragement could be easily chastised as being weak. At that very moment, however, the Lazy Trail Saloon would serve as a different testimony.

***

Alvin Wong sat at what became the most popular table in town that day. It wasn't because of his renowned image though; it was because of who he was with.

Marcus Hipple had returned from their fishing trip a changed man. Always hungry for positive change, he took Alvin's advice at the campfire and did some soul searching.

Since their last encounter, he thought about the reaction others gave him when he came on too strong and about the times he bored someone to tears by trying to get them interested in what *he liked*. He spent time looking at his high school senior picture and then

67

compared it to who faced him in the mirror. *Who is that guy anyway?* he questioned while pointing at his reflection. It was a wake-up call for Marcus Stanley Hipple that made him start the first day of the rest of his life by just being *himself.* The enlightened man would go a step farther and wear clothes that matched the location and era he was living in. That, along with washing his hair to its natural look worked like a charm.

Not only did his first attempt to ask the lovely Miss Katie Kaiser out for coffee yield success, he was also being noticed by others in a more favorable light. Marcus rallied to the occasion by exposing a humorous side that was always there. In essence; he was now that popular new kid in town.

Equally important: he didn't sacrifice any of his already- known good qualities. Always true to a fault, he had with him his friend, Grant—another guy who was simply misread a bit. An individual who was absolutely, totally, without any doubt- *just fine.* That evening, many gathered around to share the laughter that carried down the street while getting to know Marcus and Grant better.

The result? Another fishing trip planned that would bring close to half the town! Alvin fueled the fire by saying, "It's a good thing that I'm a judge. We're going to be making a lot of noise on this trip!"

***

Unbeknownst to the township, Blaine Wolf was on deck and marched to the office he had recently stormed out of. Upon entering the practice, he faced Wilson Peets and said, "I need help."

68

15

———— •●• ————

Dr. Wilson Peets had Blaine Wolf sized up from the get-go. His experience with such characters that exerted an over- confident nature usually had them walking out, only to return later. The professional played the odds and left Blaine's file open. As luck would have it, Wilson's schedule allowed him to be admitted at once. That, along with the big man apologizing for his recent outburst, suggested that there might have been a tad bit of spiritual intervention as well.

The doctor-patient team cleared the air with an understanding that caused Wilson to laugh. "That happens all the time," he said. "What's important is that you're here."

Blaine got comfortable on the familiar padded couch as he watched the therapist review his notes. At that moment, he began to feel vulnerable as if he was an insect for a science project. He reverted to his nature and became overly cautious, like a curious cat watching from a distance.

Wilson sensed the man's apprehensiveness and delicately asked him an introductory question—an appetizer that would set the stage for bigger and better things down the road. He asked Blaine how he viewed his identity. Taking a deep breath, the rancher rolled his eyes and gave a generic answer to the generic question. This told the doctor that the patient was just as normal as anyone else. Eventually, Blaine's comments resulted in a conversation that ranged from sports to favorite fishing spots. Soon a few high school stories were exchanged, with laughter ensuing. It was like sitting with a friend at a football game. Finally, there was a long enough pause for Wilson to ask, "Is there anything specific that you'd like to talk about?"

Blaine was in a jovial mood and said, "I'm sure there's lots, but I can't think of anything right now."

"Great," came the response. "That means that I can have my

69

lunch now." Both men laughed.

Blaine stood up and asked, "How much do I owe you?"

"For visiting with you?" he asked. "Just find a good cause and give how you see fit." He then added, "I'd like to see you again and probe a bit deeper."

Blaine's first session of professional counseling was a good experience, leaving him game to go another round. An appointment was made, followed with a firm handshake and gratitude. "I never thought that I'd like it here," he said. The rancher left feeling a bit lighter, stronger and more confident.

It was fresh on his mind that he still owed the counselor through a different means. Blaine wasn't about to let it plague him like the dollar he owed Gary and decided to swing by the local church on the way home to give a donation.

Within twenty minutes, Blaine entered the quiet sanctuary. With hat in hand, he walked down the aisle that led to the altar. In plain view, front and center of the pulpit- was a metal box with an opening on top that a standard-size letter could slide through. He opened his wallet and dropped a twenty-dollar bill into the container labeled "Donations".

Immediately, he was startled by the voice of Pastor John. "We certainly appreciate that, Brother Blaine."

The cowhand flinched as if an ice cube was dropped down his back. Turning around, he saw the holy man in the dark robe and said, "Geez, you scared me!"

"Sorry about that," said the pastor. "I promise to be more quiet next time. Are you in a hurry?" he asked.

The two sat in a pew to visit. Blaine mentioned the session he had with Wilson Peets and thanked the pastor for, once again, giving sound advice. "He's a good man, isn't he," commented Pastor John.

"I'll have to agree," replied Blaine.

It was Pastor John's move. The clergyman was poised and determined to make sure that Blaine Wolf's pursuit of happiness would include the Lord. Decades of counseling was about to be unloaded on the rancher who needed to look *beyond human help*.

Serving his own appetizer to entice a future main course, he asked a subtle question: "Tell me, Blaine. Do you ever feel that something very simple- but sacred is held back from you?"

In a bar, such a vague question would have him pay his tab and leave quietly. Sitting next to Pastor John while in church was a totally different matter, however.

"I don't understand what you're talking about," he replied

quietly.

Scratching his head while looking at the ceiling, he squinted and tried to explain what he meant. "What I'm trying to ask you is, *have you ever felt let down at a special moment because you didn't get what you felt you were deserving of?*"

"Like not getting what you wanted for Christmas?" remarked Blaine.

"No, not that," replied Pastor John.

Blaine thought a bit and grasped another concept. "You mean like having it rain on a fishing trip?"

"Well, something like that," responded the pastor. "How about a once-in-a-lifetime sunset where everyone can see it *except for you*- even though you're right there with them?"

"That's perfect!" replied the holy man as he patted Blaine on the back. "Has there ever been something absolutely God-given that you felt was spiritually being kept from you?"

Blaine now understood the question and concentrated with his mouth open. For a spell, he could only draw a blank until a distant memory came to light. "My mother used to tell me that our land smelled like heaven when God smiled on it," he recalled in soft words. Looking at the pastor, he elaborated further. "She would go into great detail describing the enriched fragrances that blended through God hand's when He wanted us to smell His kingdom. She said that it was a sign that He approved of what we were doing. I knew that my mom was telling the truth, but I could never smell it the way she could." Lowering his head, he said, "I thought God was mad at me. In fact, I still do," he admitted sadly.

Looking off in the distance, he gave a slight laugh when another memory came to mind. "I remember this beautiful dress she made; it was two shades of yellow, like an Easter dress. She would wear it on special occasions and flap her arms up and down, as if she were flying, while saying, *"I'm a butterfly; aren't I beautiful?"*

A tear trickled down his cheek as he reflected deeper. "Those were the happiest times I've ever known. She was such a beautiful woman, and I miss her dearly."

Silence followed with the holy man finally speaking. Placing a Bible in Blaine's hand, he said, "Why don't you keep this? It has lots of good messages from our Lord and guides us through our most troubled times."

Without any hesitation, Blaine accepted the gift and said, "Thanks. I'll look through it when I have time."

16

—•••—

Nightfall arrived at Eagle's Lake with a campsite getting a little out of hand. With the exception of some gray hair and outdated fashions, it had the look of a high school party- minus the keg.

Generally, this sector of adult males walked through everyday life in an orderly fashion. Tonight would prove to be a bit different, however. Word got out about the whopper Marcus recently caught and the good times shared camping. The local bar would have to wait another day to have good business. The guys decided to let their hair down and head for the hills!

It was an hour before sunset with fish on the grill, horse-shoes under way and a controversial card game with ever changing rules. *"It's always been that way!"* shouted one old cuss to another.

Off in the distance, a cluster of swaying branches gained attention.

Soon all conversations were silenced as the fellowship watched what appeared to be two ghostly figures from a past century wander out of the brush. There, in plain sight, they stood in semi-tattered clothing with wild, overgrown eyebrows and long beards. A closer look showed angry, weathered faces with tobacco-stained teeth and piercing eyes. There was also an important element that could not be overlooked: each held a shotgun with a finger on the trigger.

Wide-eyed and petrified, all remained quiet and attentive. The stare down lasted for what seemed to be an eternity, until a voice with a familiar twang spoke out. "Do you realize how much racket you youngins' are making out here?"

The angry hillbilly then puffed on his corncob pipe and waited for an answer.

Sheriff Merle Emerson Chesterfield immediately recognized the perturbed resident and called out, "Is that you, Zeke?"

The mountain men knew the long arm of the law when they heard it and instinctively dropped their weapons. They now resembled grade school children in front of a principal. They smiled ear-to-ear, with hands behind their backs, as Zeke McDonald gave his reply. "Look, Sheriff Chesterfield. That fine I owe you for hunt'n possum out of season is in the mail…I swear!"

"There's no lawman up here today, just a bunch of guys fishing," said the sheriff in a friendly voice.

"He's telling the truth!" said Alvin.

"I don't see any public officials around here," called out Marcus.

Laughter broke out with Zeke and his friend, Emmett feeling welcomed. "Well, ya better make some more room," said Zeke. "Ya got two more a-comin.'"

Introductions were made, with Emmett giving a friendly pointer. "I'll show ya all where the catfish are hiding," There were no longer any locals who could complain about the louder-than-normal campground. Soon a sky full of stars enticed Zeke to play his harmonica to the delight of everyone.

Marcus was sitting next to Alvin when his cell phone rang. It was Katie Kaiser *again.*

Until recently, Marcus wondered if he would literally give his right arm to have her hand. When his friend Alvin told him to just be himself and present her with the *real* Marcus Hipple- he did just that. In essence, he peeled himself like an onion. When Katie saw who he really was and realized that he also held the highest position in town, she became goo-goo eyed over him. The town beauty set her sights on the dashing young mayor by cooking dinners, meeting him at coffee shops and dropping by to see what he's up to.

The attrition rate took its toll like kids in a candy store. If his phone wasn't ringing, he could sense her presence nearby. True, she was the apple of his eye for much of his life, but still, he was beginning to feel as if he were married and forgot to report home. Staring toward the universe, he recalled a piece of age-old advice: *Be careful what you ask for—it might come true.*

His recent surge in popularity placed him on top of the eligible bachelors list in Hangman—a title a young man *thought* he would want.

"That's the third time tonight!" exclaimed Alvin.

The young mayor couldn't discuss the matter with his friend because he was being summoned *again.*

"Yes, dear," he would say in a sweet voice. "Of course I care," he would say in a defensive tone.

Alvin patted his friend on the back, saying, "You poor guy…"

His normally happy-go-lucky face was now beet-red with embarrassment. With his cell phone pressed against ear, he once again excused himself to find a more private setting.

Looking at Zeke and Emmett, Marcus wondered if it was time for him to consider a career move...

\

17

⸺ •●• ⸺

Blaine Wolf united with his family on a mission of remorse. The man of the house was now of a more passionate temperament and gathered everyone in an emotional group hug that lasted over a minute. While kissing each member on the head, he apologized for his recent behavior and lifted the curfew he implemented. He then said the magic words: "Everyone get dressed. We're going out for dinner!"

That evening, the Wolf household was one of happiness, with a night life of their own ready to happen.

The Lazy Trail Saloon was virtually empty because of the last-minute campout at Eagle's Lake. This was probably a good thing because the family would have drawn stares from the peanut gallery. Blaine, along with his wife and children, enjoyed a delicious meal. They even shared a massive ice cream dessert with four spoons—a free-for-all that almost became a frenzy.

Rejuvenated with family pride, the foursome unanimously agreed that a stroll through town would be fitting.

"Can we go to the library?" asked Teri. "My class has artwork displayed there, and I did one that's really cool!" The young girl's idea was perfect. It had been too long since Dad had attended a parent-teacher conference or expressed an interest in his children's school life.

"I'd love to see that!" exclaimed her father.

The Hangman library was a historical monument all in its own. It was a Gothic brick structure surrounded with ivy and tall pillars. At night, it lit up the entire block from original lamps converted to electricity. Inside, shiny floors with high ceilings and plaster walls served as an echo chamber that held a century worth of secrets.

Blaine marveled at his daughter's painting. To him, it was clearly the best one on display. The bright colors she used gave a perfect contrast of the storm clouds over a horizon. His little girl had painted a picture of their ranch that displayed great feeling and emotion.

The proud father picked her up while kissing her cheek and saying, "I'm so proud of you!" He set her down and looked at his son. "It's like how you play baseball," he added while giving a thumbs-up. "It's just perfect."

Junior was happy that he wasn't left out.

There were many exhibits strewn throughout the library; the Wolf family made an evening out of it. Soon each wandered a different direction with Blaine discovering something that caught his interest. At the end of the hall was an easel that held a reader board. It served as an open invitation for a seminar about the town's history that was taking place. *I've got to hear this*, thought the proud rancher. He entered the room where those present immediately turned with stunned looks. It was well known throughout the valley that all discrepancies involving the early days of Hangman centered around the *Wolf family*.

"Well..." said the local historian, Heidi Best. "It's appropriate having you join us this evening, Mr. Wolf."

Blaine was all too familiar with the Amish-looking woman who stood at the podium. The tall, slender body and the tight, rigid face and steel-blue eyes had never changed since he knew her. She too, was a direct descendant from settlers who helped establish Hangman. She was also the Wolf family's worst critic. The elegant senior, whose gray hair was always in a tight bun, had Blaine in her crosshairs- and she was staring right through him.

Blaine's throat became dry like the desert, causing him to take a deep swallow.

"I was just going to cover our town's history of water rights and easements," she said with a gleam.

"Are you still complaining about that?" asked the native with arms stretched out. "That issue had been resolved before any of us were born!" he exclaimed in his baritone voice.

"Resolved?" laughed the historian. "It was always dodged when it came time for a court date and eventually fell by the wayside, like squatters' rights."

"We were never squatters!" he yelled. "We were the first ones here!"

"Your family arrived with others," the retired school teacher rebuked. "Let's move on," she suggested. She stood back to reveal a drawing of the town on a blackboard. It was as if Blaine was meant to be there that evening—at that time, in that room.

Her illustration was accurate, showing the town's boundaries and the handful of ponds scattered about. Most importantly, it clearly showed the brook that served as a property line with several public outlets—until it reached the Wolf homestead. At that point, it was enclosed, as it passed through their acreage.

Blaine viewed the woman as an old crone whose purpose was to take every measure possible to discredit his family name. Her intent was to realign the Wolf property rights so that no one had exclusive access to the town's main water supply on both banks. "It runs through the entire town," he pointed out. "That brook has always supplied everyone."

"Originally, your property was the best and probably the only place to get fresh water around here," she said. "It was the prime real estate, where the town was meant to be centered around—until your family fenced it off and laid claim to it."

"It was finders keepers!" he shouted out. "We were the first to arrive before anyone else, and that's where we staked our claim!"

"I've heard many stories from my grandparents," she said. "They told me that there were times when your family actually charged money to families who needed access to get water or to head to the plains," she accused.

"Well, I was told different," he said in defiance. "I was told that there were those who wouldn't develop their own land and tried to take advantage of those who did!"

On that note, he knew to leave before his temper got the better of him. Blaine thought about what Heidi said and immediately had a vision of the precious coins that were hidden in his barn. He could only laugh at that point and walked merrily down the crowded hall in search of his family.

One thing for sure came from Miss Best's lecture: Blaine knew to defend the property his great-great-grandfather claimed. He would maintain his policy about letting only family and select friends on their soil. He would also keep the gates closed when not entering or leaving.

***

The following day Blaine woke up before the sun. What was normally work reserved for Gavin now rested on his shoulders. It would prove to be a long day of counting cattle and clearing land to extend his pastures. Several times he had to rest in the shade, longer than before. At sundown, he was a tired man who knew deep inside that he missed his friend and hired hand, Gavin Woodley.

After dinner, he went straight to bed asking himself, *was it really worth firing Gavin?*

18

———•●●———

Ric Bratton slid Blaine's mug to him, saying, "Watch out; it's hot."

It was a break in the action for the rancher who was without a hired hand. Reaching out with a blistered hand, he picked up the mug and tapped Ric's. "You're too good to me," he said in a soft voice. The rugged cowman then pressed a hand against his shirt pocket to verify that the dollar he owed his friend, Gary was there and ready.

Blaine Wolf's life had been an anxiety-filled three-ring circus as of late. On one hand, he felt tethered to a leash until he paid his friend back. On the other, he was viewed by possibly the entire town as a hidden charity case that was struggling to survive. Throughout it all was the ever present controversy about his heritage in regards to *who* actually arrived first and *if* their land was wrongfully attained. To stir the pot more unfavorably, he made matters worse by publicly shaming one of the most beloved men the county had ever known. In a frivolous lawsuit, he single-handedly denied Gavin Woodley his honor and abruptly terminated his services. An equation that amounted to open sores and lack of sleep. Paranoia accompanied him on this journey. Like a wanted man, he tended to lie low while nervously touching the pocket holding the bill he owed. He also acquired a peculiar habit that had the man on edge periodically: surveying his surroundings for friend or foe.

Ric could sense that his friend was a roller coaster that ranged from self-doubt; to trigger-happy assumptions. In a friendly tone, he initiated what he felt would be a good subject. "Hey, I missed you at the camp out the other night!" he said tapping Blaine's shoulder. "I was hoping to sit next to you at the fire."

The camp out was news to Blaine; *nobody mentioned a thing about it to him.* "What camp out?" he asked while setting down his mug.

Ric's face clouded with the realization that the some-what impromptu outing simply hadn't reached Blaine in time. Slapping a hand across his forehead, he said, "We forgot to... I mean that I forgot to..."

Blaine took over. "Don't worry about it. I'm sure that nobody wanted me there anyway." Feeling dejected, he placed some loose change on the table and left with Ric not knowing what to say.

The main reason why Blaine Wolf went to town was to keep his appointment with Wilson Peets. His recent visit at the general store added more insult to the injuries on his already-full plate. With eagerness, he arrived at the practice and patiently waited his turn.

When entering the confined quarters, his mind was already made up in regards to what he wanted to talk about. The accommodating therapist was glad that Blaine arrived with a list he formulated all on his own. This showed that he was serious and wanted to go forward. "That's great!" said Wilson in a complimentary voice.

Blaine started with events that happened most recently and went backward. He told of the all-guy campout *that excluded him.*

"Maybe it was an oversight," he commented.

"They would have noticed my absence," Blaine retorted. Next, he mentioned the town library holding a seminar designed to paint a false picture about his family.

"Go into further detail," requested Wilson as he took notes. Blaine's knuckles began to turn white as he reiterated what Heidi Best accused his forefathers of doing over a century ago. "She wasn't even there when this town was settled!" he cried while shaking his fists. The man on the couch went farther back and mentioned that he keeps such undesirables off of his property to protect what's rightfully theirs. "I even started to close our gates again," he said with authority.

Wilson leaned back in thought and asked his patient a profound question: "Do you think that the community revered your property as somewhat sacred, and possibly regarded your family as aristocrats?"

Blaine folded his arms and stared upward. In a smug voice he said, "We do live on the highest elevation in town..." Turning toward the psychiatrist, he pointed his finger, adding, "It's the most beautiful spot on this entire earth, and it was there for us to build a life!"

"Who knows," said the doctor. "Your homestead might be viewed as the Mount Olympus of Hangman.

Blaine reached up to clutch the sky. He liked how the compliment was worded and could only agree. "Now that's a good way to put it…" Wilson was taken by those words as he studied the man's pride. Wisely, he left that statement alone and addressed another subject that was closely related: the difference between being strong and being weak.

Blaine had a lot to say about strength versus weakness—so much that he didn't know where to start. "One thing that I absolutely hate is when someone tries to force a gift on me," he said while shaking a finger toward the ceiling.

"Any experiences on the matter that you would like to share?" asked Wilson.

Fresh in his mind was the casserole left on his porch. "They couldn't credit me for supporting my own family," he said.

Wilson had an interesting concept to point out: "Do you think that they were just caring neighbors who held a great respect for you and your family?"

"That gift also included information from the welfare office, and that's just going a bit too far," he said sarcastically. There was more. He mentioned the money Sheriff Chesterfield insisted he take with tips on where the best food banks were located. "I know that he meant well, but that guy doesn't understand." Then he recalled his family receiving charity away from home. "Did someone run an ad in the paper?" he jested while turning his hands palms up. "Even before this mess started, there was a time when my bird-brained nephew and our so-called mayor tried to give me a Christmas present."

"Did you accept it?" asked Wilson.

Looking straight at the man wearing the white uniform, he replied, "No, I don't want to get that started!" Blaine rattled off a few more accounts of when he refused to be the recipient of receiving anything from anyone that he didn't want to be close to. "They are just trying to set me up for a favor they don't deserve," he concluded.

Wilson changed the topic to a more acceptable subject that tied in: his mother.

"I am under the impression that your mother was a generous, compassionate, gift-giving person," speculated the doctor.

Blaine sat up and said, "Was she ever!" From there, he recited countless stories of when she cooked, gave, helped and shared with people in need whom she didn't even know."

Wilson knew his business and asked a strategic question that would put a different spin on things. "Did she ever let others on the family property; people who weren't considered family or close friends?"

Blaine's face tightened, with a shade of red beginning to show. "That's the only complaint I have about my mom," he said in a trembling voice. "That woman's heart was so big that she would do anything for anyone. There were times when I thought that families passing through were going to live with us. In her world, *everyone else came first.*"

Dr. Peets extracted a lot that session and wanted to put a close on it. He did that so Blaine wouldn't have too much to digest between appointments. He merely wanted to establish a pace that stayed even with his daily life.

Blaine was all too willing to schedule another appointment. He took the next available opening and asked, "How much do I owe you?"

To his surprise, the session was a piddly fee of only thirty dollars. In gratitude, Blaine paid in cash while making a vow. "Do you know what I'm going to do?" he asked Wilson. He answered his own question: "I'm going to give a donation to a worthy cause like you had me do last week."

The doctor liked what he heard. As they shook hands, he smiled at Blaine, knowing that deep inside, there was a good heart. "That sounds good to me," he said. "See you in a few days."

***

Blaine's departure from Wilson Peet's office would be a carbon copy from the last visit. He would once again go to the empty church and put currency in its donation box.

"Your mother certainly raised you right," projected the voice of Pastor John. That comment hit an iron that was still hot. At that moment, Blaine realized that he was giving above and beyond—*the way his mom used to.* It was a different kind of feeling that he wasn't accustomed to, but it made him feel good inside.

The stockman wanted to transponder the emotional momentum he was feeling. He and the pastor sat down in the same seats where they last visited and opened up.

Blaine remembered that he was talking to an adult male from the community and asked a question. Wincing at the holy man, he cautiously asked, "Hey, did you by chance attend that shindig the other night at Eagle's Lake?"

Utilizing a humorous side normally hidden, Jonathan answered by asking a question. "Now, Blaine; who in their right mind would invite a man of the cloth to an all-night guy thing?"

Blaine was shocked to see that the preacher had a funny side.

"You're all right!" He laughed while patting Jonathan's shoulder.

"I try to be," he volleyed back.

The visit escalated into what could only become a friendship. Humorous stories were followed by more and then more, as they echoed throughout the sanctuary. While they were catching their breath, the pastor asked Blaine if he had a chance to look at the book he gave him. The rancher felt a shade of embarrassment and gave a common answer. "I've been meaning to," he said.

"When you have time," Pastor John said in a calm voice. It was then when he said something that specifically pertained to the session he had earlier. "It's nice to give, but it's much richer when it's accepted. When you took the Bible and seemed happy about it, I felt that we both got something."

Blaine froze as if Wilson was the preacher and Jonathan was the therapist. Small talk finished the visit with Blaine leaving the church having lots on his mind...

19

---•●●---

Across the street, Judge Alvin helped resolve what he felt was a minor discrepancy that should have been settled over a barbecue.

"This doesn't make any sense," said the man wearing the robe. "If you two always had an understanding- then why change it after all these years?" Using his non-intrusive methods, he elaborated further by asking a common question. "Look, you guys are fishing buddies—did you two even *try* to discuss this matter?"

Lynn Hatten looked at his neighbor, Wade Walker, in shame. The lean, blond-haired, blue-eyed man bowed his head. The husky man with a dark crew cut did the same. Together they realized that the hedge that had always served as a property line between their two estates had never before been in question. Through time, each land-owner noticed that little by little, the multitude of ferns and bushes were lessening their backyards. Each observed that the other was encountering the same phenomenon. To put it in a nutshell: *the plants were growing equally on both sides and were overdue for a thorough trimming.*

The result?

All charges were dropped, with Lynn's wife, Cynthia, suggesting that they celebrate their friendship with a backyard barbecue to begin at once. The bubbly brunette with rich-brown eyes started to jump up and down while clapping her hands.

"That's a great idea!" agreed Wade's wife, June. The petite woman with red hair pointed at Alvin, saying, "And *you* are invited!" Handshakes were exchanged between the conflicting neighbors who wanted their friendship back. It was agreed that after the meal, the men would join forces for further assessment of the property line issue.

"Well," asked Cynthia as she looked at Alvin. "Can you join us for an early dinner?"

"I have no more cases today," he responded. "You bet I'm coming!"

Leaving the steps of the courthouse, Alvin spotted Blaine. *"Hey you!"* he yelled with a pitch of authority. Blaine couldn't help but hear him as he approached his truck. "I'm ordering you to attend a barbecue with us right now—or you'll be in *big trouble*, mister!"

Blaine could only laugh. Turning around, he raised his hands and said, "Okay, I'll go peacefully!"

Next, Alvin attended business by asking Lynn if he had an extra steak. Like everyone else; how could he not love Alvin's diplomacy? Laughing hard, he looked at the congenial man and said, "We've got plenty and would love to have Blaine join us."

Alvin called out to Blaine, who was still across the street, and said, "It's at Lynn's place. Let's follow them in your truck." "Sounds good to me," replied Blaine as he open the door to his four-wheel drive. "Get in here!" he ordered while motioning his arm.

The drive to the barbecue became an intimate moment between the two men. Something was bothering Alvin, and it pertained to his friend, Blaine. He would use that opportunity to get it off his chest.

"Blaine, I think I owe you an apology," said Alvin.

Blaine was gobsmacked to hear such an admission from a classy friend who was always a positive force. "About what?" he asked.

"The other day, a group of us were talking about the overnighter I had with Marcus at the lake."

"I heard he caught a big rainbow," commented Blaine. "Did he ever!" exclaimed Alvin. "It was good too," he added, referring to the cookout. "Anyway, some of the guys were at the Lazy Trail and we started talking about it. Next thing you know, we're kicking around the idea of going back up there in a large group. It all came up so quick," he pointed out. "I assumed that every guy around knew about it and would naturally be there. It hit me hard at the campfire that everyone thought that I would let you know about it. I really messed up- and I'm sorry. *You* would have made it even better."

Blaine heard what he needed to hear. Most importantly, it came from the right source. He knew that Alvin was his friend and would always look after him. At that moment he felt an emotional weight leave his shoulders.

He responded by telling the truth. "Oh, don't worry about that." He chuckled. "I took my family out that night, so I would have had to turn it down anyway. I promise to make the next one, though."

"There will be lots more," replied Alvin with a touch of excitement. "I promise!"

Blaine suddenly remembered that his wife, Stacey, should know that he would not be coming home soon. As he was reaching for his cell phone, it rang. It was Stacey telling him that she and the children were invited to a play after school that would have an array of food following. "It's a social meant for the seniors at the Community Center that we just got invited to," she explained.

"Well, that sounds fun!" he said gingerly. "The three of you should go and make a night of it."

"Are you okay fending for yourself tonight?" Stacey asked.

"Okay?" he questioned in a humorous tone. "I was just invited to have dinner with Alvin and some friends. I'll probably have more fun than you will."

Alvin heard what Blaine said and gave him a huge thumbs-up.

"Okay, I love you too," the proud family man said while disconnecting the phone.

***

Blaine was starving when his medium rare steak was served. That, along with June's blue ribbon baked beans, Cynthia's family potato salad, and corn from the garden, had him drooling. Dinner was a typical country setting. It was outside near a fire pit, with enough seating for everyone. Despite his controversial reputation around town, Blaine was still treated like family.

This was definitely a contrast for the man who never allowed his hosts to set foot on his property.

Compliments to the chef circulated, along with interesting stories and giggles. After the meal, Lynn and Wade inspected both sides of their property line to discover that it was Mother Nature who had played a trick on them.

"Can you please forget that I ever made in issue out of this?" asked Wade.

"I will if you will," agreed Lynn.

Alvin watched the exchange from a distance and could only admire what he saw.

Cynthia's hospitality ran tandem with June's. Together, they offered Blaine a tour of their yards.

"I'd love to see them," he answered.

"I'll join you," said Alvin.

What they saw was an enchanted theme that competed with Blaine's property. A freshly painted wishing well, miniature windmill and walking bridge that crossed a pond were only a part of it. The beauty continued through a vast acreage that also had a

85

pasture outlined with flowers and healthy trees. Blaine and Alvin never knew that the properties they saw from a distant road were so breathtaking.

Scratching his head, Blaine had to ask: "This is so beautiful—how do you two find the time to do such great work and still raise a family?"

"Gavin Woodley is the one to give credit to," said June. "Why, he did most of this and hardly charges a thing for it." Alvin knew that any mention of Gavin would churn Blaine's stomach, especially if it was yet another report about how honest and hardworking he was. With hands in pocket, Alvin looked away with an innocent expression while whistling a happy tune.

Blaine started to slur his speech with Cynthia apologizing that she couldn't hear what he said.

"Oh, it was nothing," he replied.

It was starting to get dark when Lynn's Aunt Claire and Grandma Rosie arrived home. The women, who shared a mother-in-law house on the property had just returned from a local play. They, along with Lynn's daughter, Renée and Wade's son, Darrell were thrown for a loop when seeing Blaine Wolf visiting their families. It was obvious by their facial expressions that many horror stories were heard about the rancher who lived at the edge of town.

Being raised right, the children, who were classmates with his children greeted him with respect. "Good evening, Mr. Wolf."

Blaine put away all rumors by displaying a warm smile. "Well, good evening to you! Did you enjoy the play?"

Astounded by the man's friendly demeanor, their eyes bulged with excitement as they began to tell him all about it. The report lasted a few minutes with the surrounding adults seeing a compassionate side of Blaine Wolf that they've never seen before.

It did come with a price attached, however.

No good deed goes unpunished.

Grandma Rosie was holding a plate of her homemade fudge that she provided for the social. The transparent cellophane revealed a defeat: not one piece was even touched—a grand insult coming from a room full of hungry children.

Looking at what appeared to be droppings from an original Easy Bake Oven, Blaine feared the worst.

"Mr. Wolf," cried out the seventy-six-year-old. "Please have some of my fudge for dessert."

At that moment, Blaine remembered the advice that came from not one, but two sources that day. Advice about making others happy because *you accepted their gift.*

After all; *didn't the grandmother's family just have him over for steak and share their world with him?*

With all eyes on him, he continued the good character he displayed by being a sport. Despite being a poor actor, he pretended to be enthused about the overcooked, watered-down mix about to enter his mouth.

"Did you really make these?" he asked.

"I certainly did," she said with a smile.

Placing the treat in his mouth, he chewed what resembled a tough piece of meat and almost swallowed it whole. She held another unwanted piece, insisting that he enjoy it as well. He repeated the process, saying, "That was good, but I can't eat another bite."

Blaine was telling the truth.

"I'll let you take some home," she said.

Naturally, she looked at the popular judge and gave him the same offer. Alvin was quick on his feet and told a good lie. "Oh, I can't. It's a Chinese custom that no one from an Asian ancestry can touch chocolate after sunset."

It worked like a charm—leaving more for Blaine. Alvin's audience nodded their heads in admiration as if to say, *"That was pretty good!"* With the exception of the baker and one guinea pig, all were on the same page holding back the laughter.

The ride home had Alvin express concern for his friend. "Should we stop by the store and get some Pepto-Bismol?

***

Blaine Wolf went to bed that night mulling over the day's events. His travels illustrated that at least *some people* were willing to accept him. Still, he felt that their estate was being threatened by certain townsfolk, and that fear justified him keeping his gates closed.

What was important was the one-day-at-a-time factor. He came home to a happy family. They loved the play and told him all about it while he acted surprised, wanting to hear more...

Blaine extended his heart further. It bothered him that Grandma Rosie had poor baking skills; *or could it be the ingredients she was using?*

The following day, he went to Ric's store to buy baking products that his mother always swore by. *"You can't go wrong with these,"* she would say while picking a box off the shelf. The shopping spree had an additional bonus: Ric had since gathered himself and taken full responsibility for not reaching out to his friend for the camping trip. "I should have gotten in touch with you first thing!" he said with great sorrow.

Blaine had since gotten over it and said, "If I was more like you, *everybody* would have told me." He then winked while talking about the outing he had with his family the same evening. "I couldn't have gone anyway—not that night."

Ric was relieved.

Blaine left implementing a new habit his counselor taught him. For the first time ever, he put a small donation into a dressed-up soup can labeled 'Saint Jude'. Ric did everything he could not to cry as he admired the big man leaving the store.

Within twenty minutes, Blaine was at the front steps of where Grandma Rosie lived. Upon opening the door, the cattleman took control. "Good morning, Rosie! If you have the time; I'd like to invite myself in and trade baking secrets with you." The most tactful approach to improve her fudge had been administered.

The woman, who never had anyone ask about her kitchen skills, almost fell in love. "Oh, that sounds fun!" she said. "C'mon in!" The bakers started off with teatime. Rosie was never quite sure about how to interpret the imposing figure that sat before her—until now. A conversation took place where the old gal reminisced about having tea parties with his mother. "She was such an exquisite host," said Rosie. "Back in those days, there were more of us and we rotated where we would meet," she said while holding a porcelain cup. "We were all in agreement that your homestead was by far- the best place to spend an afternoon." The old woman then made a comment that registered deeply. "It was just incredible to meet there," she added. "It always smelled like we were at the gates of heaven."

Throughout his childhood, such comments were made with him pretending to savor the fragrance others raved about.

There were other memories he had about his mother when she had friends over. "I remember hearing you ladies tell stories about your grandparents," he said as more stories unfolded.

Soon both were in the kitchen wearing aprons, with the new baking supplies alongside the old. "Would you mind showing me what you normally use to make your fudge with?" he asked. Rosie pointed at an old box with a faded label. Picking it up, he squinted his eyes to read the expiration data. "Well, here's your problem right there!" he said. "This box should have been thrown out years ago."

The kind old lady was from the *old school* that knew it was a sin to waste food. She mentioned that with Blaine having an answer. "It's not being wasted at all," he said. "Once the shelf life expires, it should be used as fertilizer for your garden. The good earth loves to eat that stuff up, and it grows a better crop for the family!"

The problem was solved with the stock being rotated! Working as a team, they measured the right amount of water and poured the mix into a large bowl. "I was taught long ago to add chocolate chips and walnuts to the batter. It makes it richer," he pointed out.

Later that day, after sprinkling her garden with the outdated perishables, they soon found themselves sampling Rosie's new recipe on her back porch. "My goodness," exclaimed the visitor after taking his first bite. "This fudge will be the first to go!" he said, implying the next community social.

Rosie patted her heart as she leaned back, looking off in the distance. *Finally, I can bring something I can be proud of!* she thought.

The visit with Rosie covered a good portion of Blaine Wolf's day. Before leaving, she presented him with a gift that took weeks to make. "Our knitting club has been thinking about you," she said.

Blaine was caught off guard and realized that he was still considered by many as being a charity case that was slipping below the waves. He also knew that his mother's friend had her heart in the right place. Utilizing all his strength, he put his pride aside and listened to her.

"We know that you're a good hardworking man who has fallen on hard times," she said. "We were working on a project but didn't know what to make, or who to make it for. It was Betty Carson who mentioned your situation to our group."

Blaine's face contorted upon hearing a name he vaguely knew. *Betty Carson?* he wondered. *Isn't she the assistant manager at that diner two towns over?*

Rosie chose the best words she could find so as not to taint her newly-formed friendship. Once finished with her informal presentation, she handed him a white vest with purple and pink embroidery. What possibly started out life as a blanket was rushed into service by being converted into a manly XXL vest.

"Why don't you try it on?" she asked. Blaine used the same diplomacy he displayed when offered fudge the past evening. Knowing how happy it would make her, he put the uneven garment over his shoulders and slid his arms through the openings. "Oh," she cried out. "You look so good in it!"

He thanked her several times for the thoughtful gift *and left a better man.*

On the way home, he stopped by the night box to mail a letter at the post office. While sliding the envelope into the mailbox, Mrs. Driscoll drove by and stopped to do a double-take on the fashionable vest he wore. She left, with him knowing that soon many phones would be ringing.

Blaine stopped caring about what the old bitty thought and was proud to wear his new gift. Laughing to himself, he began to wonder about those who did care too much about what others speculated. He recalled the many humorous stories his friend, Ric shared about what he had been accused of. More rumor mill stories came to mind like when he himself was labeled a violent man- or his present battle having masses question if he was in the poor house.

Once he even overheard in a conversation at his son's Little League game, that *his family was held captive in their own home.*

***

At his next session, the middle-aged man shared his recent experience with Grandma Rosie.

"That's wonderful, Blaine," exclaimed Dr. Peets. "You made others happy by allowing them to give!"

Blaine was on a roll and mentioned the nosy woman in the community who constantly talked about him.

"What about?" asked Wilson.

Blaine clasped his hands behind his head and looked up. "Where do I start?" he asked in a sarcastic tone. At random, he gave one episode after another. Finally, he gave the most recent one about wearing the awkward vest with bright colors.

"It seems to bother you when she paints a picture about your interaction with others," observed Wilson.

Blaine thought about what was said and gave a response. "I guess that's what she's doing."

Dr. Peets placed his pen and notebook aside and addressed a broad topic. "Let me ask you, Blaine; what's the single most important aspect about your entire life?"

Blaine responded with the obvious answer. "My family."

The seasoned therapist had a question he always wanted to ask. Poised and in control, he fired away, "Do you interpret Mrs. Driscoll as accusing you for treating others—including yourself– better than the way you treat your own family?"

Wilson scored a direct hit. Blaine tensed up as his memory released an avalanche full of guilty verdicts. Wilson drove the point a little further. "What you did for Grandma Rosie—does your wife also need the same support?"

Blaine saw the light and began to tremble. He now realized how negligent he had been to Stacey and needed to make up for lost time.

***

That evening, Blaine picked flowers from his property and presented them to his wife. He then said, "I love you, honey," and kissed her.

After dinner, he praised the wonderful meal she prepared and asked her afterward to join him in his truck.

Together, they drove just outside the gates, where he put the vehicle in park. He got out and instructed her to slide over into the driver's seat. Once there, he fastened her seat belt and he was soon sitting where she normally rode. Pointing at the brake pedal he said, "Just press your right foot down hard enough to keep the truck stopped..."

20

————•●•————

It was a busy sunup-to-sundown workweek for the fatigued rancher who was beginning to lose weight.

Tending his land and sharing brief, quiet evenings with his family became the only life he knew. That, along with weekly shopping and keeping his appointments with Wilson Peets, kept the rancher in question out of the public eye. It was in town when Blaine saw an incident that made his life stand still.

He noticed Gavin at a gas station with his family. It was apparent that he was having an altercation with three strange men who could have passed as professional athletes. Blaine watched from a traffic light as one of the men pushed him. The former employee, who was under 150 pounds sopping wet, held his ground to protect his family. This gained the respect of his assailants who extended their hands as a way to make peace. The episode ended with handshakes and the waving of hands when they left in their car.

Blaine saw a tactic used that was superior to how he handled things when he was younger. It came from a mild-mannered individual who always seemed to handle things *right*. At that moment it hit him hard that it was possibly Gavin teaching *him* a lesson. Blaine spent the rest of his day consumed by what he just witnessed.

Before bedtime he was in the barn with Blue's wagging tail. He gazed at the many artifacts that chronicled his family's arrival in Hangman- to the present day. Vintage hand tools, framed pictures and the almighty wagon that brought them to the *New World* were all within sight. On a nearby table lay the Bible Pastor John had given him. The one he said he would look at when he had time.

A voice inside told him that *he had time.*

Sitting at an old desk that once belonged to his great-grandfather, he began to mull over the ancient writings at random.

Certain passages jarred memories from his Sunday school days, others from past church services. On occasion, a familiar quote he heard from his mother would surface. It was all good stuff that seemed to reroute him down the path he was *meant to follow*.

A calling that came from Jesus of Nazareth Himself.

Tired from a strenuous workweek with a few curves thrown in, the rancher fell asleep with the good book in hand. Such was the setting when Stacey entered the barn to check up on her husband. It was the greatest sight she had ever seen! Testimony that she had made the right choice 'hanging in there'.

***

The following morning, Blaine was hard at work clearing land. He was near the family plot and felt a compulsion to take a break and pay respects.

The headstones seemed to be standing at attention as if they were watching the fifth- generation continue their heritage. As always, he picked wild flowers that grew about and gifted each relative. When it came to his mother's stone—she got the 'treatment'. Several fresh flowers were placed on top of older ones. It was there where he always said his prayer for her, the entire family- and to God.

The loyal son then took a deep breath to see if he could smell God's kingdom the way his mother used to describe it. To his disappointment, no such spiritual intervention was granted. At that moment he noticed a yellow butterfly on a branch- that seemed to be watching him. "I bet you can smell Heaven," he said to the insect.

Blaine then went back to sweat under the hot sun.

***

The following day, Blaine was on Wilson's couch discussing the event at the gas station. "I thought that his family was going to watch him die..." he said.

Dr. Peets listened attentively to the story. He then asked Blaine his opinion in regards to how he saw Gavin handle himself.

"He was brilliant!" he said. "He held his ground and ended up with them basically apologizing to him."

"Why was that?" asked the doctor.

Blaine thought a while and gave an answer: "Because they liked him."

93

Gavin Woodley would become the day's topic. Blaine was comfortable talking about this usually sensitive subject. He was asked if he considered him a friend. "A friend?" asked Blaine. "He's more like a son," he said. "I'm so proud of that guy!"

From there, many stories were shared about the hired hand who never asked for much; the one who always went above and beyond. "That guy knew when to tackle a chore before I got around to assigning it," he added. "And he always showed up early," he said shaking a finger. "Don't get me wrong," said Blaine. "I love my son, Junior; but Gavin and I have worked long days together when the others were at school."

It was Wilson's time to inject an obvious question. "Then *why* were you so hard on him about the time when his truck broke down?"

Blaine stared upward with a blank expression on his face. Finally, he turned and looked directly at the man taking notes. "I don't know…"

***

It was a few days later when the hardest hit in Blaine Harold Wolf's life was delivered.

Blaine saw a little girl with her mother selling campfire cookies when he was in town. Like anyone with a family, he respected what the child was representing and wanted to show his support. The nine-year-old recognized him and started to walk backward, saying, "Go away, you're mean!"

Blaine stopped in his tracks with his mouth wide open. "What do you mean, little girl?" he asked.

"My mommy told me that you won't let any of us see the rest of heaven because you're mean!"

"Heaven?" he questioned while making a nonthreatening motion.

"Mommy says you have a piece of heaven all to yourself and that we aren't good enough for you," she explained.

Before he could discuss the matter any further, she commanded, "Go away!"

The fourth grader's mom stepped in with a verbal assault. "Mr. Wolf; haven't you caused enough trouble for one day?"

It was the worst pain the rancher had ever felt in his entire life.

***

The next few days had Blaine working long hours, spending

94

evenings with family and reading more spiritual passages in the barn. The temperamental rancher couldn't deny that he was getting more and more drawn to the new/old book he was given. As time passed, he delved further into the verses of inspiration and began to share them with his family. The Bible was elevated from man cave status- and graduated to family time. "Junior, could you read this paragraph and tell me what you get out of it?" he would ask his son.

"Teri, if you have a moment; I'd like to read something to you that has really left an impact on me," he'd say to his daughter.

Home life was taking a turn for the better. The television set didn't play as much and the barn became uninhabited. "Why don't you look through this and see if there is anything you would like to share with the family?" he'd suggest to his wife.

There was more.

The ritual of horseback riding as a family became more frequent and Stacey soon acquired a driver's permit.

Blaine still had issues on his property. He was certain that there was a movement to take his land, thus making him adamant about securing the gates. He also realized that, to many, he was a pariah—or even worse; a charity case. Most recently, the heaviest weight had been added: the Campfire girl who knew of him as a bad person—a nightmare that played in his head over and over again with each playback magnifying the fear he saw in the child's face.

Blaine would find temporary peace from remembering the words of encouragement he always got from Pastor John. He would also think about the nurturing sessions he had with Wilson and how it all made sense scientifically.

Temporary remedies at his command that would carry him between visits. This particular night was different, however. He didn't have the inner strength to endure his heavy load any longer.

Virtually, he was in an emotional tailspin and wisely called both Wilson and the pastor. He was fortunate enough to have each answer their phones so late. They were happy that Blaine knew to reach out at such moments and agreed to meet him at John's church the next day at noon.

God is good.

Blaine basically knew what he wanted, but didn't know how to acquire it. The frazzled rancher then tried prayer. Alone, he knelt down and clasped his hands. With all sincerity he asked our Lord to allow him to live in a town that matched how wonderful his home life had become.

I hope I'm not asking for too much, he thought.

Blaine was on the right path.

21

———— •●• ————

The following day, Blaine was sitting with Wilson Peets and Pastor John. The three sat at the altar with their chairs forming a circle. Blaine knew that he was around trusted friends who had the credentials to discuss the social and spiritual turmoil he was going through.

"For some reason, I wanted to be with you guys *right here*," he said, pointing down at the carpet. "I just can't explain it," he continued with open arms. "It's as if I'm supposed to be here at this very minute..."

It was at that precise moment that Blaine found his answer. The doors from the main entrance opened, casting sunlight down the center aisle. The three men turned to watch a tall silhouette approach them as the light disappeared.

In silence, the figure marched directly toward them. "Welcome, my brother," greeted Pastor John. "How may I help you today?"

The stranger, who drew nearer, turned out to be no stranger at all. "God bless you, Pastor Jonathan," responded a graceful flow that needed no introduction. It was then when a large African American man, with a smile as large as life, stepped onto the altar.

"Pastor, Ellis!" cried out Pastor John. "It's so good to see you!"

"Well it's so nice to see you, my friend," he replied. "And who do we have here?" he asked while extending a hand to Wilson.

The counselor stood up and introduced himself while shaking hands. "My name is Wilson Peets, and it's a pleasure to meet you, Pastor Ellis."

"Nice to meet you, Wilson," said the seventy-one-year-old minister.

Wilson sat back down. Turning to Blaine, he recognized the man he once knew as a child. Taking a step back while placing a hand over his heart, he cried out. "Oh my Lord! Is that you, Blaine?"

Blaine felt *spiritually right*. He knew beyond any doubt that his prayer for guidance was being answered. Standing up, he could only give the man who served his mother's final ceremony a hug. "You came here for me; didn't you, Pastor?" he asked while shaking with emotion.

"That must be it," said the holy man as he patted Blaine's back. "I woke up this morning smelling a godly fragrance that engulfed my entire surroundings. It didn't take long for me to realize that your homestead is the only place I know that carries a 'gates-of-heaven refreshing scent'. From there, I knew to travel here at once."

Blaine sat back down as Pastor John nodded at him with encouragement.

Pastor Ellis pulled up a chair and joined the circle. Gazing at Blaine, he said, "I remember your mother. She was a God-send if I ever met one!"

"Yeah, Mom was loved by everyone," replied Blaine.

"I remember that pretty yellow dress she wore on occasion," recalled Pastor Ellis. "There were times when the entire community was in your backyard, just past your barn, for a Bible study. She would often wear that dress and flutter her arms saying, "I'm a butterfly; aren't I beautiful?" The pastor slapped his knee saying, "It was so beautiful because back there, she did look like one!"

Blaine laughed with a full understanding. "Everyone started to call it her 'butterfly dress' and would sometimes ask her to put it on."

"Yes, yes," agreed the pastor. "In fact, she once mentioned that she wanted to meet the Lord in that dress and made me promise that when her time came, she'd be buried in it."

Blaine remembered the day his mother was taken as a tear trickled down his cheek. He also knew that what the reverend was saying was gospel.

"She was a remarkable woman who definitely led others to God," commented Pastor John.

Wilson remained quiet as he absorbed what was being said.

Pastor Ellis continued his path down memory lane. Laughing to himself, he said, "I remember the day I asked you what you wanted to be when you grew up, Blaine. Remember that?"

A little smirk telegraphed that he knew exactly what he was referring to. "You mean Santa Claus?" he asked.

"Yes, Santa Claus!" confirmed Pastor Ellis.

"I still have that dream," admitted Blaine.

Wilson saw a rich part of Blaine's inner-self being exposed and tactfully touched off on it. "What do you mean by being Santa Claus?" he asked.

Blaine was not embarrassed to explain what he meant. Looking at the three whom he considered friends, he began to express himself, barring no holds. "I wanted to keep Christmas going," he said with enthusiasm.

"How would you do that?" asked Wilson. The three men leaned back to listen to his answer.

"I would arrive in my sleigh during the middle of the day and take all the children to the North Pole!" he said.

"What if all the snow melted until next winter?" asked Pastor John.

Blaine's eyes grew with excitement as he explained things in further detail. Leaning forward, he gave his answer. "Our family wagon is the sleigh!" he revealed. Using hand gestures, he described the entrance he would use. "I would enter town shooting candy from my six-shooters! The children would pick up the candy as I would fire more from my barrels. When all of the candy was picked up, they would know to climb in for a hayride that was full of more candy and shiny coins! And then they would have the gift of a lifetime. I'd take them back to the North Pole with me!" he said with a glimmer in his eye.

Wilson immediately asked an obvious question. "How can you get your wagon to the North Pole?"

Blaine stood tall with arms folded and said in a noble tone, "Our property is the North Pole!"

"Wow!" said Pastor John, in a faint breath as he leaned back holding his forehead.

"What happens next?" asked Wilson.

Blaine had an answer. Looking at each man, he grew more excited and painted a picture of what he always wanted. "When we arrive, they would see a campsite with enough tents for them and all their friends. There would be plenty of trout poles near our ponds and horses that we can ride on all day! At night, we'd have a barbecue and fish fry, and watch the stars come out around the campfire!"

Blaine took a deep breath and raised a finger. "Then comes the best part!" he said.

"What?" asked Pastor John.

"What is it?" asked Wilson.

"Please tell us, Blaine," pleaded Pastor Ellis.

Blaine's face was tense as he eyed each one of them. "It's something my family started to do recently that has changed my life forever." Suspense started to build while Blaine concentrated harder, trying to find the right words to better explain.

Looking at Pastor John, he said, "We would then start to read out of that Bible you gave me."

A long pause followed.

Pastor Ellis could see the child he remembered and followed his logic. "Your place would make a great North Pole," he said. "For as long as I can remember, everyone always wanted to have our church events there. Bible studies, special services- even weddings were once held there."

Blaine began to act dignified. It was as if he was a king. Pastor Ellis then turned the tide. "One day the Lord took your mother and it all seemed to stop," he said. With soulful dark eyes, he stood up and held Blaine by the shoulders and asked, "What happened?"

"They were moving in on our property to take it!" he answered. "Our mom was just in serving the Lord," he said. "But she could be too nice, and soon we had more and more people entering our property and staying longer."

"Are you talking about the campouts that the Campfire program was allowed to have and her tea parties?" asked Pastor Ellis.

"I'm talking about all of it!" he said in a raised voice. With a smug expression, he continued. "That wagon train wouldn't have survived if we weren't leading it," he pointed out with conviction. "That entitles us to have the first choice of property rights!"

"Calm down, brother Blaine," said Pastor Ellis in a soothing voice. "I know this town's history by heart and nobody is trying to railroad you."

Blaine was getting beside himself and ran off on a tangent. "I suppose you know Alvin."

"Judge Alvin?" Pastor Ellis asked in a high pitch. Looking at the three European descendants, he said, "We know each other very well and *do* share a few things in common."

His comment went over their heads.

"Alvin would be the first to know if there were any legal property disputes over your land," said Pastor Ellis. "I can rest assured that the small talk is only that—and will never escalate into something else. Besides, this is an established town where everyone seems proud to be right where they are.

It was Pastor John's turn. "There is one complaint that does circulate on occasion."

Blaine took the bait and asked, "What's that?"

"At one time, there was a family that did such a great job caring for others that the entire town would make a pilgrimage there just to further worship our Creator. In fact, the entire community was unified there as if the town were being settled for the first time..."

Blaine's knees buckled from the choice words that took him

back to his forefathers.

Pastor John had more to say. "Because of that very family, now everyone shares their land at one time or another throughout the year to keep that church tradition alive. Every family except the one that started this ritual..."

Blaine took a dry swallow, being fully aware that it was the *Wolf family* he was referring to.

"Have you ever noticed the old Bible in the town museum?" asked Wilson. "It's credited for having traveled with the wagon train that brought the first settlers."

"In school we used to take field trips there," replied Blaine. "I know what you're talking about."

"Blaine," called out Pastor Ellis, "it's town history that the settlers read from that very book every night. It goes without saying that your family had held it many times." Leaning close to the rancher, he emphasized a fact. "It's the same words that your mother read at her Bible studies on your property—the very ones that you are now sharing with your wife and children."

Blaine looked up realizing that there was a common thread from the town's origin- to his present home life. An obscure twist lay somewhere, causing something to be out of kilter.

"Nobody is trying to take your land," Wilson assured him. "They just want you to be a player when it comes to church activities like all the other families do in their backyards. A great tradition started by the town's first family," he reminded.

The frightened little girl came to mind. Blaine found the courage to share that story as he fought back tears. "She said that I was mean because I wouldn't share a piece of heaven."

Pastor Ellis took a side. "She was right! She knows that this entire town is to be shared like heaven—including your property."

It was all coming together fast. Pastor John then delivered the knockout blow: "You were probably meant to be this town's Santa Claus, and the Lord needs you and that sleigh."

Blaine stared into the vastness and felt an epiphany. His guidance was now coming down from up above- and he knew what to do. Looking at Pastor John he asked a question. "Do you have any more of those books that you gave me?"

"Enough for everyone in this entire town plus a few extra," he said with a wink.

Blaine factored the information in his head and abruptly left, knowing that he had to answer a *calling*.

22

———— •••• ————

Blaine drove from the church to the bank and bought fifty dollars worth of rolled-up coins. Next, he went to the store and bought almost an equal amount of candy.

"Looks like you're throwing a party," commented Ric.

"That's a good way of putting it," said Blaine. "I don't have time to talk, but I'll call you later," he added while leaving the store.

"I'll be waiting for your call," Ric called out.

There was plenty of daylight left when Blaine parked his truck at the closed gates that sealed off his domain. He stared at the metal barrier as if it were Satan himself denying entry. Moments later, he returned with a welder. He opened each gate far enough to where it touched the antique frame. With determination, he welded them entirely open, as if he himself were knocking down the Berlin Wall.

It was at that moment that he was granted a gift that always eluded him throughout life. A gentle breeze flowed through the entryway that would never be closed again. One that tickled his nose in a most endearing way. It was the full fragrance of everything absolutely beautiful in God's natural world that stimulated all of his senses. The everlasting breath of life that his mother always spoke of. This enlightenment put spiritual winds in his sails, granting him more strength to do what he was called to do.

To accomplish what he was born to do.

With the North Pole now open for passage, it was time to address the sleigh. Blaine had rolled the well-preserved wagon many times and treated the wood when necessary. He took handfuls of hay and spread it throughout the cargo area until it was cushy enough for young passengers. Next, he sprinkled the coins and candy evenly throughout and stood back.

Something was missing. The enlightened rancher scratched his head while trying to put his finger on it. Pacing about, he thought about the multitude of instances that ruffled feathers and the visits he had with Ric, Pastor John, Wilson and others. There was something forgotten—but what?

Finally, he remembered the night he took his family out and ended up at the library. It was there where he temporarily sat in on a seminar about the town's history, only to be chastised by Heidi Best. One of her complaints was about the coins that his family charged to cross their property.

Without hesitation, he retrieved them and placed the precious metals on a wooden table. Immediately, he got a sick feeling in his stomach. The coins reflected an evil side of mankind that should have never been collected. Just then, a thought entered his mind. *He should let the descendants from those very families reclaim them.* He grabbed a few coins and mixed them in with the newer currency and sweets. He continued until the last ones were freed.

Last, he harnessed Trigger and Annie Oakley to the sturdy wagon that migrated his family over 150 years ago. Santa's sleigh was now ready to go, with lots of toys for good girls and boys. Before embarking on the trip, he called Stacey on his cell phone. "Honey," he said with an air of excitement, "I have an idea."

"What is it?" she asked in a curious tone.

"Look, it's Friday night," he said. "It's been too long since we had friends over. Tell Junior and Teri that the weather is perfect for a campout and that they can invite as many friends over as possible."

"That sounds great!" Stacey replied. "Are you feeling okay?" She laughed.

"This man has never felt better in his whole life!" he said. "Have your friends over too, and I'll invite mine."

The well-kept Studebaker product was ready for action as he sat tall in the seat, calling, "On Trigger! On Annie Oakley!" In the blink of an eye, it began to roll forward in an even rhythm. Modern-day technology aided the revived relic as he left his private road and turned onto the thoroughfare.

Today was Blaine's turn to guide the prairie schooner, and he did so as if five generations were assisting in every step. The land cruiser from a past century turned heads while making a simultaneous clomping sound that echoed throughout. Jubilant bystanders were rewarded, with Blaine throwing candy in return and tipping his hat.

Phones started to buzz, with many people running out their front doors to watch the spectacle and catch their favorite chocolate bars. By the time he rode into town a crowd had already formed, cheering him on! Tiny bags of jellybeans flew everywhere as Hangman's first mode of transportation stopped in front of the Lazy Trail Saloon. It was at that moment when Blaine pulled off another surprise. He wore a holster that carried two six-shooters that could only fire blanks. Firing the harmless popping sound into the air, he formed a faint cloud of smoke that lingered above.

The crowd went nuts!

Blaine's arrival couldn't have happened at a better time. It was Friday, and school had just let out. Citizens young and old were now roaming town, looking for anything to do. "So you really do have that wagon!" Alvin Wong cried out.

"We have more than that!" Blaine assured him. "Let's get as many children as we can get into the wagon, and everyone can follow me to our place. We want to have a community bonfire tonight and have everyone in town there! There's also a lot of fish to be caught if anyone's interested."

"Is this a campout?" asked Mayor Hipple.

"It sure is," replied the rancher. "And *anybody* can stay for as long as they'd like!"

"I'll spread the word!" promised the mayor.

Blaine looked at Alvin and patted the seat next to him. "Get up here!" he yelled. "I need someone to ride shotgun in case there's any trouble along the way!"

Many were within earshot and howled with laughter. "Hold on, I'm coming!" said Alvin.

Soon a wagonful of children was searching frantically through the hay, as candy and heavy coins turned up. Sitting proud, the rancher guided the town's first set of wheels to the first claim ever staked. Alvin gazed at the distant hills. It then occurred to him that they were traveling on the first wagon credited for crossing those very mountains.

He was speechless.

Upon entering the modified entryway, another gust of heaven's scent engulfed the travelers. It served as further confirmation that the proud man was indeed on the right track. Everyone on board felt its grace, with comments being made.

"Wow!" exclaimed the Chinese American. "I've never smelled anything so pure in all my life!"

"That's because it is life!" responded Blaine.

The rest of the family was behind the barn. Together, they were in a state of wonder, not knowing what happened to their front gate or why the wagon and two of their horses were missing.

There was also an obvious question that needed to be answered. Why did the man of the house suddenly invite the entire town over that day?

It became prevalent as to why when a friend of Teri's pointed at the parade entering the homestead: "Hey, Teri; look what your dad is doing!"

103

The mother and two children, along with their friends turned to see the horse-drawn wagon stride toward them. If that wasn't a big enough surprise, Blaine could be seen by all, wearing a smile as wide as a canyon.

Soon all were all sitting on logs that surrounded an old fire pit. Naturally, Blaine was the focal point and broke the silence. "Well, don't look at me. I only live here!"

His humorous remark was greatly received, causing an uproar of laughter. Needless to say, his son was proud and called out to him. "Hey, Dad, do you want my friends and me to get some wood and start a fire?"

Blaine looked at the empty pit and threw his arms up in the air. "Well, doesn't that sound like me?" he asked. "I invite everyone over to share a bonfire with us—and I don't even have one!"

At that moment, a new voice entered the group. It was Ric Bratton with his wife, Shannon and their son, Sean. The proprietor of the town's only grocery store was pulling a shopping cart full of hotdogs, buns, condiments, chips and several cases of pop. "Make it a good one, Junior, because we have lots of hot dogs here!"

Blaine immediately had an idea: "If anyone wants fresh trout, we've got the poles…"

Faces lit up as Stacey got to her feet. "All fishermen, and *fisherwomen*, follow me!"

Ric wasted no time and walked up to Blaine, saying, "Scoot over, mister. You didn't think I was going to miss out on this one, did ya?"

"I would have dragged you here if you were!" he replied while getting his friend into a playful headlock.

More heavy hitters arrived. Pastor John, Pastor Ellis, and Wilson Peets brought the church station wagon which was full of Bibles. "We brought these along," said Pastor John waving a book in each hand.

"Great idea!" said Blaine. "Those things have what it took to open my eyes."

"Well, good," said Pastor Ellis. "Don't mind us; we'll start passing them out."

Blaine noticed a familiar child approach him in a campfire uniform. It was the same little girl who expressed hatred toward him not too long ago. Her distaste for Blaine had obviously subsided, as she handed him a box of cookies. "My mommy says you are a good man and we want you to have these."

Blaine looked at the box and said, "Mint cookies? I love them!"

Her mother spoke next, saying, "We apologize for the other day. We are grateful that you have allowed us over, and we hope that you enjoy the cookies."

"The other day?" laughed Blaine. "That was a lot nicer than how most people greet me!"

Out of nowhere came Grandma Rosie. The newfound friend was holding an empty tray. "I'm glad you got those mints," she said. "My fudge disappeared within a minute!" she said with pride.

"Well, you and I will just have to make some more!" exclaimed Blaine.

Looking beyond, he saw Marsha Greene with her two daughters. They were friends with the girl in uniform and her mother. They saw the jolly man and ran over for a group hug. "It's so nice to be here," said Marsha. "Everyone knows that the town was started *right here* with your family."

Heidi Best joined in by showing a few precious silver dollars she and a few mothers received from their children. "You're absolutely right about that!" she said. "If this good man's family didn't come here when they did, this town would only be dust." Leaning forward, she kissed him on the cheek, saying, "I always knew you were a great man who would do the right thing."

Blaine blushed as more townsfolk addressed him.

A surprise guest called out as if they were long-lost friends. "Blaine!"

He turned around and was somewhat amused to see that Mrs. Driscoll had found her way. "Long time no see," she called out while waving frantically.

Eager to bury the hatchet, he replied, "Why, hello, Mrs. Driscoll! Why don't you get over here and let me give you a great big hug?"

Stacey, as well as the entire county, knew of Mrs. Driscoll and admired how her husband made the renowned gossip feel accepted.

A flow of personalities continued to address the man of the hour.

"Do you mind if we give ourselves a tour of your property?" asked Aaron Nelson, who sat next to his wife, Dorothy.

"Not at all," replied Blaine. "I want everyone to feel at home."

"Your place is beautiful!" commented Grace Kinney.

"You'll have to thank Gavin Woodley for that," said Blaine. "In fact, where is he?" he asked while looking around. With his former hired hand nowhere to be seen, he pulled out his phone and began to dial.

The stage was now set: the very people who watched Blaine diminish Gavin's dignity in court were all present—including those who heard about it. The reformed rancher was now honing in on a set of spiritual dominoes that were about to fall in order. A reverse rotation where wrong would now be righted.

The humble laborer had just entered the property after having been told several times that *everyone was welcomed to spend an evening at Blaine Wolf's place.*

"Hi, Blaine," greeted the polite voice who never complained about his work. "I was told that we were invited to come over. We certainly appreciate this!"

Blaine turned around and looked at the man who worked harder than *he* ever did. The guy who was always first to start and last to leave. Blaine's eyes met Gavin's, compelling him to give his 'other son' a massive hug. "Where have you been?" asked the property owner. "I've missed you!"

"I knew you were sore at me," he explained in an apologetic tone. "I just wanted to make sure that I was never in your way, that's all…"

"In my way?" questioned the rancher as he waved his arms. "Look at me," he said while taking a step backward. "What you usually do around here has been making an old man out of me. I learned the hard way that I can't run this place without you."

Gavin was vindicated in front of the township. He fought back a tear and said, "I'd love to work for you again."

"You better," replied Blaine, resting a hand on Gavin's shoulder. "I'm slowly losing my grip around here trying to do it alone."

It was now Gavin's turn.

He reached into his pen pocket and produced the check for two-hundred dollars he wanted to give his former boss at the right time. "Please take this," he said. "It would mean everything to me, and then we can start over."

Blaine looked at the good man and saw him in another light. With pride set aside, he accepted the check and felt a remarkable weight being lifted from his shoulders.

"When do I start?" asked Gavin.

"Look," said his friend, "you know more about this place than I do. Start anytime and let me know what needs to be done."

The entire valley heard those words as the partners were once again united.

The dominoes continued to fall.

It was after those powerful words when Blaine felt a tapping on his back. Turning around he saw his neighbor Gary, giving him a look that only a friend could give. "Hey!" he said. "Where's my dollar?"

The elusive bill had been all but forgotten because of the trials and tribulations Blaine had recently faced. Reaching into his pen pocket, he felt that it was still neatly tucked away and waiting to be returned to its rightful owner. Pulling it out, he handed it to his neighbor in one motion. "You mean this?" he said as he growled like a wrestler.

Taking back his dollar he said, "Yeah, like that!" Gary growled back and pretended to throw a punch.

"Ya better watch it," Blaine threatened. "I have a judge on my side!" All present laughed as additional weight was lifted off of Blaine's shoulder.

It was then when he would receive another gift in life that he was always denied. He saw his nephew, Grant and Mayor Marcus Hipple. They were with his mother and beautiful fiancée, Katie Kaiser. All joining in on the fun! Directing his attention to them, he commented, "I just wish I was smart enough to accept the gift you two tried to give me during the holidays."

Marcus spoke up. "It's still in my car; I'll go get it." He got up and returned shortly with the belated Christmas gift.

The Santa Claus in Blaine Wolf liked it. "Well," he said to his audience. "As far as I'm concerned, every day should be Christmas!"

"Open it up," requested the nephew.

Blaine unwrapped the gift to see that it was a framed butterfly exhibit with a miniature butterfly net thrown in. At first, he didn't know what to think and took a long pause. "Well, you guys certainly go all out. Where did you catch these anyway?" he asked.

"We didn't," replied Marcus. "We went to the thrift store to find a frame for a picture I had and saw that this was the same size."

Blaine was interested in their story and wanted to hear more. "Well, what happened?" he asked.

"Read the names credited for catching each butterfly," said Grant. "This is what got us interested in them."

Blaine inspected the array of colorful wings that were separated into five groups with names written underneath. Looking closer, he read each name and gasped. All five were of women from his family line; from his great-great-grandmother- all the way down to his mother. Each was credited for which butterfly she caught years ago. What was striking was that his mother was documented for having caught only one. The very one, beyond any doubt, that was the most beautiful being displayed. It was a bright yellow butterfly that matched her signature dress.

Blaine was almost petrified with the realization of why she was so fascinated about being a beautiful yellow butterfly. Almost stuttering, he asked the experts a question. "I have seen a butterfly like this one around here before," he said while pointing at it. "Could they be related?"

"They would all be related," said Grant. "That's because they're all from the same colony."

Everyone watched in silence. They took turns looking at the display and knew exactly what Blaine was talking about.

Blaine looked at the judge who sentenced him at his own request and could only love him for it.

Alvin winked back.

The man who once believed in a separation of classes had seen the light. *"That's because we're all related,"* said Blaine Harold Wolf.

"Amen to that!" cheered Alvin.

Everyone followed suit with a huge "Amen!"

At that moment, an identical butterfly flew by catching Blaine's attention. Without thought, he followed it with his new net as others watched. It traveled gracefully until it came to rest. Delicately, the rancher positioned the net in hopes to catch it. It was at that moment that he felt the closest he had ever felt to God and froze. The butterfly had landed on the very tombstone where his mother lay.

Through the Lord's hands came another fragrance of His mighty kingdom, further blessing the child who now understood. The immaculate butterfly turned to look at Blaine while spreading its rich wings. At that moment, a revelation took place enabling him to hear the words his mother always said: *"Look at me; aren't I beautiful?"*

***

The trials of Blaine Wolf's life was much like the fragmenting tumbleweed he noticed during his moment of disparity. There was something different about that bush, however:

It once held precious berries from its vines, personifying the early days of the rancher's life.

What was once a thriving bush that produced fruit would now have a second coming by spreading its seeds in a rotating fashion. With the aid of much needed rain and the grace of our Lord, it would flourish once again, yielding more berries than ever before.

EPILOGUE

---•●•---

The story you have just read personifies an age-old battle that brings forth a travesty.

The separation of classes.

The ultimate social injustice that depicts an ideology which utilizes rumors seasoned with stereotyping—propaganda that dictates *who* will get cuts in line and which ones are to be outcast...

All based on the natural differences that the good Lord has blessed us with.

The town of Hangman is an all American, close-knit community that illustrates this point. From sunup to sundown, all walks of life can be seen walking through town and greeting one another. Things change in a heartbeat when one sticks their head into a beauty parlor or barbershop. Unless your unannounced arrival causes the room to silence at once, you'll be hearing some pretty interesting stuff about a neighbor you know quite well...

Sadly, family heritage, income level and even ethnic background are all subject to attack. Flashbacks soon dance in our head, causing pain to fester out questions that need to be answered:

How many times have we known of a kid who got chastised by classmates for simply being the "who" that they are?

What about that guy (or gal) from work who is excluded by the 'in crowd' because they were too honest to compromise their identity?

Or what about a certain clerk or server who's a little odd and pays for it socially?

We can throw in police officers, preachers, teachers and elected officials too.

Fortunately, there is a cure-all. In fact, it's a simple remedy that has always been at our fingertips:

Prayer.

Reaching out to our divine Creator through the unity of a good

109

old-fashioned Bible study has always sobered up the best of 'em—placing all of us on an even playing field! Through prayer and strong faith, goodness is promised to prevail—*whether you're a prominent rancher or a beautiful yellow butterfly.*

Matt

AUTHOR BIO

Laura Shea with her dad, author Matt Shea

Matt Shea is a developing author, having published nine books. He is greatly inspired by the writings of Andy Griffith and focuses on the common folk that small towns are made of.

He credits the success of his first book, *The Groundskeeper And Other Short Stories,* to his family. The values that were instilled throughout his childhood gave him the strong sense of justice that is conveyed throughout his writings. The Shea family is only an average American family from an average neighborhood. Their secret is that they are close-knit and accept others.

Matt's mother, Vyerl, set an example of being self-sacrificing, having never placed herself first. She always cared about the feelings of others, no matter who they were. She even sponsored many foster children despite having a family of eight. During the holidays, the Roman Catholic mom had been known to have a Hanukkah bush for their Jewish friends. There were even years when the family would make Christmas gifts and personally deliver them to seniors in rest homes.

Many of Matt's friends are senior citizens or foreign-born. He has the common practice of brewing a pot of tea and inviting them over to watch Alfred Hitchcock. Together, they will watch Alfred, share a cup of tea, and listen to his manuscripts afterwords. Sometimes, these social gatherings last well beyond midnight.

"This is where I get most of my ideas," says Matt. "I learned this from my mom."

Matt Shea appreciates all who take the time to read his stories. He even has a site, where many free stories in their entirety are available, and extends his email address for those who have any comments or ideas. Matt knows that through other people he can expand as a writer and a person.

Matt Shea
www.mattsheabooks.com
www.worknmatt7@aol.com

Matt Shea Books:
(http://www.mattsheabooks.com)

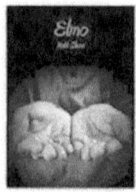 Elmo

 Lauratown and other short stories

 The World's Greatest Rock Star And Other Short Stories

 The Groundskeeper And Other Short Stories

 Chase: A Special Person & The Discovery of Teddy Downing

 The Meadowdale Community Project

 Chase: A Special Person

 The King of Coalman's Hill